About the Author

Kay Ni C was born and reared in Dublin, Ireland. She is the mother of two brilliant sons, of which she is very proud. She always loved history and myth. So much so that when she received a history essay for schoolwork, she couldn't just stop, and she would write on and on past the asked word count. Stories have always been passed down through their family, and she would love others to enjoy and feel a connection with what she writes about and her home. She is a huge animal lover who wishes to one day be able to help rescues as much as she can.

Tribes of the Gods Endure

Kay Ni C

Tribes of the Gods Endure

Vanguard Press

VANGUARD PAPERBACK

© Copyright 2024
Kay Ni C

The right of Kay Ni C to be identified as author of
this work has been asserted by her in accordance with the
Copyright, Designs and Patents Act 1988.

All Rights Reserved

No reproduction, copy or transmission of this publication
may be made without written permission.
No paragraph of this publication may be reproduced,
copied or transmitted save with the written permission of the publisher, or in
accordance with the provisions
of the Copyright Act 1956 (as amended).

Any person who commits any unauthorised act in relation to this publication
may be liable to criminal prosecution and civil claims for damages.

A CIP catalogue record for this title is available from the British Library.

ISBN 978-1-83794-265-7

This is a work of fiction. Names, characters, businesses, places, events and
incidents are either the products of the author's imagination or used in a
fictitious manner. Any resemblance to actual persons, living or dead, or actual
events is purely coincidental.

Vanguard Press is an imprint of
Pegasus Elliot Mackenzie Publishers Ltd.
www.pegasuspublishers.com

First Published in 2024

Vanguard Press
Sheraton House Castle Park
Cambridge England

Printed & Bound in Great Britain

Dedication

To my sons, who always kept me going and supported me in finally putting my words to paper. To my mother and my adopted father, who also helped and supported me in writing this first book. They are always my rocks. To my collie, Shep, who recently passed, who was always my cuddle when things were not great.

Acknowledgements

To the Pegasus Publishers Team, who believed in my book and have been amazing throughout.

Introduction

This story is based in parts of Galway, Mayo, and Meath. It is a fictional mythological story about the hidden secrets of my home and the Irish people.

The Tuatha De Danann: Ancient Gods of Ireland. Long forgotten, rarely spoken about, passed down from generation to generation through old story tellers in local pubs. The protectors of the people and their land. A fighting spirit that they passed on to their descendants.

Aes Sidhe: Fairies, magical protectors of all who live in nature.

Bru na Boinne: Ancient mystical monument older than the pyramids. Secrets hidden within magical corridors to the afterlife.

Ui Breasail: An island that is only ever seen from a distance and can never be accessed by humans. It only appears to the eye of humans once every seven years before disappearing into a mist. The exact location is still unknown.

Fomorians: Beastly creatures who cause death and destruction long since banished to the depths of the sea.

Chapter 1

Fergus rushed across the yard of the castle. He had overheard a disturbing conversation between two men tonight.

There was talk of revenge on Tiernan, their Chieftain and Tuatha De Danann. He heard words akin to a witch and great hordes soon to be arriving on their shores. Sweating, he rushed through the pathways, trying to make his way to the main hall, when he felt a pain in the back of his head, and blackness overcame him.

The two men whispered in the corner and watched their unconscious prisoner intensely. Fergus slowly came around, feeling the thumping in his head. His eyes were blurred, blocking his vision of the figures who were hidden in the dark.

They continued to whisper before crossing the room to where he was tied up.

When their faces came into focus, Fergus stared in disbelief. "What are you doing? Why are you doing this?" he asked in a shaky voice. He knew these men.

They had eaten with him and his family many times. His mind was racing, trying to understand the treachery. Neither man spoke; they just stared at him with deep hatred.

Dian stepped up, smirking at Fergus, lifting his sword in the air and before Fergus could even let out a scream, Dian cut his throat in one swift strike.

Dubh laughed a little, watching the blood squirt out. Fergus's eyes widened, knowing he was going to die as his gurgled chokes echoed through the room.

Dian leaned in close to his arm and bit in as Dubh joined in. Fergus's eyes, now full of death and horror, began to shake uncontrollably as his eyes glazed and his head slumped over, taking his last breath. Dubh punched Dian in a fit of frustrated anger. "You ruined the fun, Dian; I wanted him to feel it," he continued, "you know the flesh is tastier with fear."

A feeling of dread crept in as she crawled through the long, wet grass, mud splashing up into her face. Cold and terrified, every sharp rock stinging as they cut into her tender skin. Closing her eyes and gritting her teeth to avoid screaming out in pain. She edged her way slowly away from the shore.

The only warmth she felt was the blood dripping along her skin.

Straining her ears, listening for any sign of danger, she moved like a rabbit evading a predator.

No moon or stars in the sky tonight to help find her way. A veil of black surrounded her; only a thin shadow of the tree line could be seen ahead. The whites of her eyes shone wild with fear from what she had seen. They laughed as they cut him up without hesitation; she shivered in herself thinking of it.

Fiadh loved to explore, to be at one with all things wild and free. Her father had given her warnings about straying too far away from home. *I can hear him now, "I told you it would get you into trouble." How I wish I could hear his voice now, be safe within the walls of the castle.*

For a moment, she paused to catch her bearings and began to feel drowsy, shaking herself to wake.

I can't fall asleep out here; no one survives a night out in the open, she thought.

Moving a little faster, staying low and quiet, she crawled towards the tree line. A cold chill ran up her back as though someone had walked through her soul.

Tiernan looked out over the wall of the castle, his mind unsettled and worried. Fiadh had disobeyed his orders not to leave the grounds again.

He knew she always returned safe, knowing the forest so well.

Yet he worried more tonight than ever. He admired and loved her wild, free spirit and love for the animals, but he knew one day it would create a problem.

Fiadh never stayed that late in the forest. Now, with this ominous feeling he had been getting since morning, he was anxious to have her home safe.

Some of his men went searching for her before dark. They had not returned, which indicated a bad sign. Shouting came from the darkness, deep in the trees, interrupting his thoughts.

Tiernan looked into the forest from the tower; he could see torches moving swiftly in their direction.

Conn rushed out to the courtyard, shouting for the gates to be opened. Twenty men had gone out; only five could be seen returning. He moved quickly along the wall, down the half-lit spiral stone stairway to lead him back out to the courtyard.

Every step, he could hear the hustle of his men and the shouts coming from beyond the gate. He nodded to Conn as he moved back inside the great hall.

Five men ran through the gates, falling to their knees. Bloody and out of breath, mumbling how they had been attacked and the others had scattered into the forest.

Conn shouted to the men and women gathering around, "Get water and blankets now!"

They rushed away to follow his orders.

Conn is loved and highly respected amongst the people of their land, and for good reason. He is a man of great honour and loyalty; the people knew he was next in line to be a leader.

As the women brought water, they surrounded the men covering them. Conn called Fallon, one of the men, to follow him into the castle.

He stood up and moved across the courtyard with Conn supporting him. They entered the wooden doors into the main hall. It was covered in torches burning bright; a giant fire blazed in the centre of the room.

Tiernan moved across to Fallon and placed a chair out for him, his brow furrowed. Clearing his throat, he swept the hair away from his face, revealing his dark green eyes.

"What happened? Is Fiadh dead?" His voice broke a little, coughing to clear it, as he stared into Fallon's eyes, searching for an answer before it was given.

Fallon raised his dirty, pale face to look at Tiernan. "Not that we found." His eyes were full of regret and disappointment, knowing how much Tiernan needed news.

Conn could already see the relief on his face slowly turning to anger.

His voice rose to a thundering roar. "Who dares attack us in our own land?" Throwing his chair into the fire in front of him.

In the back of his mind, Tiernan was still terrified his daughter may have met with the same attackers.

For now, he had to think as a leader, not just a father, and he again composed himself.

Fallon drank some water, clearing his throat before he spoke. "We did not see who they were. They came from the trees screaming in a tongue we did not know, waving swords and cutting down three of our men where they stood. No reason behind the attack. We fought hard, but more and more kept coming at us, so we retreated to warn you. There is no sign of Fiadh anywhere."

Conn interrupted, "Tiernan, I am sure Fiadh is safe and hiding; there is no other who knows the woods as she does."

Tiernan nodded in agreement, placing his hand on Fallon's shoulder. "I am glad you have returned safely, my friend. Get some food and sleep while we prepare for what is to come." Fallon excused himself and left the hall, closing the door behind him.

Tiernan stared into the fire for a moment. Glancing back over his shoulder, he called out his orders. "Conn, double the guard on the walls and send out five men to bring the people behind the walls from the town. No torches and no horns. Tell them to move quietly and as quickly as they can."

Conn nodded in agreement and moved swiftly out of the hall, leaving Tiernan with his thoughts.

Chapter 2

Fiadh moved slowly closer to the trees; she could hear the wind howling through the branches above.

No animals called out tonight. They knew danger was moving across their lands.

Who are they? She thought to herself, what do they want?

She knew one thing: they were no friends to her.

Speaking in an unfamiliar tongue, clothed like nothing she had seen before.

She edged her way to the first tree and leaned up against it, breathing heavily, relieved she finally was out of the open fields.

Vigorously, she rubbed her skin to try to warm herself.

Earlier that day, Fiadh had been enjoying the forest, picking flowers as she made her way to Dun Briste cliffs. Such a beautiful, crisp, fresh winter day it was.

The orange and gold of the leaves on the trees, watching the giant hares dance across the fields so gracefully.

They were a constant beautiful sight since she was a young child.

She often made her way there to sit by the top and dream of what lay beyond their waters.

Today, however, when she came upon the sea, there was something she had never seen before.

Great ships lined up, and small boats landed on the shore. She did not dare show herself and watched from a distance as one fisherman was approached and cut down to her horror.

She almost screamed out loud when she saw how they had just killed him without mercy.

She knew she had to move away and get home fast. She had not planned on some of them being already landed. They were moving across the fields, blocking her way.

After realising there was no way past them until dark, her heart sank.

Sliding onto the cliffside, she hid behind a giant rock, shedding a tear for the fisherman and his family. She shivered in fear, cradling her arms around her in wait for the chance to escape.

Conn rallied the men to their posts. "Gannon, get the fastest men you know to go to the village and surrounding lands to move them inside our walls." He called to him.

"Move them fast and quietly," Gannon replied with a nod, moving quickly out of sight.

He then called the rest of the men. "Twenty of you get to the walls; the watch is doubled tonight. The rest of you get some sleep and be ready if needed." All the men knew this meant to sleep with their swords and one eye open.

They watched Conn's great stature move away from the courtyard and back across towards the hall. They knew all too well he was worried, and not just for them. He had another worry: Fiadh was still outside the walls.

Tiernan sat quietly, holding his sword, thinking of what was to come upon his country and family.

He always had been a strong and fair leader who watched out for all the people of his land. His allies in the other clans looked to him for leadership and counsel. It was time for him to call them in for a gathering.

He hadn't noticed Conn standing watching him from the door. Ushering him in, Tiernan stood up from his seat and walked towards him.

Laying a hand on his shoulder, he asked, "Have you carried out all my orders?"

"Yes," Conn replied. "The men are doubled on the walls; others have gone to retrieve the people from nearby lands and towns."

"Good, good," Tiernan replied. "Conn, it is time to call a gathering of the clans." Conn nodded knowingly.

"Send four men on a horse to each clan, north, south, east and west; they can send word to the other clans. It needs to spread fast and quietly. Tell them to avoid the main routes and travel light, stay under cover."

Conn moved quickly from the hall and across to the yard. He waved his hand to the four men by a fire warming their hands. Immediately, they stood up from where they were seated and moved to Conn's side. Their faces looked worried.

Conn spoke in a low voice, giving them their orders from the king. They all nodded in understanding and moved off to prepare for their missions. No more words were needed.

Dawn was creeping in above the land. Tiernan moved across the hall towards the men surrounding the fire. They had come swiftly from the villages closest to the castle in reply to his call.

The men all sat with serious faces, knowing there was a coming threat to them and their people. Tiernan spoke loudly, "You all know why I have called you here this early morning." He continued, "We have invaders from an unknown place, and we believe they are a danger to our country."

Conn spoke up calmly, "They have made a bad decision attacking us and killing our people." His face looked angry even though his voice remained calm and clear.

The men admired him for his bravery in situations of great importance such as this. "We must act with great swiftness and power but not underestimate our enemies."

Tiernan moved to his side and placed his hand on Conn's shoulder. Conn sat back down, knowing it was time for Tiernan to give the orders.

Looking at the strong, loyal men before him, Tiernan was fierce and resolute. "We have been invaded by men not of this land; they intend to hurt us and our people to what ends I do not know. However, we will not let them." He continued, "We must recruit every man able to fight, arm them and prepare for battle." He looked around at each face as they concurred with his orders. Tiernan continued, "Kill them all with no mercy."

"Aye," the other men regaled.

The Chieftains of the other clans left the hall to recruit and prepare for the oncoming battles ahead.

Conn looked on as they left the room. Tiernan moved towards him. "Take thirty men now and find my daughter." His eyes locked with Conn's as he held his hand to the back of his head. Conn saw something in Tiernan's eyes he had never seen before. He nodded and embraced Tiernan before moving out after the other men.

Tiernan watched the strong young man leave, feeling he may never see him again.

His fear was not for Fiadh and Conn any more. The fear was something deeper. He knew something evil was coming, and it was not just these invaders but what lay behind them that would be their greatest threat.

Chapter 3

Fiadh lay on the cover for what seemed like hours. She had managed to squeeze herself into a hole and warmed herself somewhat. No longer able to hear any noises from the invaders, hoping they had fallen into a deep sleep. She crept from her hiding place, feeling now would be her time to escape back to safety.

The night had brightened a little as the rain clouds slowly separated, making room for the stars and moonlight. There would still be cover of the dark and forest to move through.

She leaned out, adjusting her eyes to the night. Rising slowly, her eyes darted left to right before moving cautiously to the trees a few feet away.

Her heart jumped as a deer leapt from behind a tree, pausing for just a second, her eyes full of fear, staring at Fiadh before racing off into the distance.

Fiadh could still feel the thumping in her chest as she tried to slow her breathing from the fright. "Come on, Fiadh," she encouraged herself. "Now or never."

Nervously, she moved through the forest at pace.

She could no longer hear the men, and she edged her way further from the sea and sand. Fiadh looked to the sky as the little sparkling lights appeared. Her mind was racing about what she had seen, and she sighed with sadness and worry.

Moving in the dark faster, the bite of the cold air from the sea no longer stung her skin. Feeling she had moved far away from the danger, she began to feel safer.

Her heart was still pounding in her chest, and she was tired, sore and becoming weaker.

The smell of the moist grass tickled her nose as the early morning was creeping in around her.

Danger of being seen was increasing by the second if she did not get further away. She could not be sure they weren't tracking her. Out of the side of her eye, something moved. She gasped.

Stopping in her tracks, she hid down behind a tree. It was still dark enough not to be seen if she wasn't out in the open. Two men were stomping through the bushes ahead of her.

She dropped to her knees and began to pray. "Please, Cernunnos, protect me from these invaders who would harm me, your child of the forest." They moved fast, beating the undergrowth hard as if they were searching for someone or something.

They moved closer and closer, shutting her eyes and holding herself up tight against the tree in the hope they passed.

She whispered her prayer over and over again, "*~Cernunnos, lord of warriors in the land of the Tuatha De, god of balance, frightening, fair, you who all look to for strength, you in whom all turn to for protection, my* *prayer goes to you to clear the forest, to make my journey safe, to remove all obstacles from my path."*

Her breathing slowed as she felt a quiet calm come over her. As she whispered over and over her prayer, her mind drifted into another place.

She could hear every blade of grass move, the bugs moving through the earth, the birds' wings catching the wind as they flew through the sky.

Deeper and deeper, her trance became. The air felt light on her skin as she could hear them get closer and closer, every footstep as it pressed down the grass beneath their feet and the sting of their swords cutting the undergrowth.

She could hear something else moving from afar in the forest. With a rushing sound, it moved swiftly in her direction, barely touching the grass beneath it. The sound moved closer and closer to her and her pursuers. As she fell back against the tree, it sailed over her around the tree and onwards towards the danger.

The screams began to echo all around her, but she did not open her eyes to look. Snarling and growling rang through her ears. She was untouched by it. She felt surrounded and protected.

Their screams to her were a distant harmony, not in the same world. Soon, they became nothing more than gurgles as they faded until they were no more.

Slowly opening her eyes, she was met with two big eyes staring down into hers. She did not feel scared, but she did not dare move. Cernunnos answered her prayers, and she was safe. The majestic image that stood before her was one of the myths from her childhood that she never imagined she would ever see.

His ice-blue eyes fixed on her intensely, yet she felt complete familiarity with him.

His gigantic head towered over her, long silver fur shining in the light from the strands of sunbeams streaming through the trees above.

He is almost as big as a horse, she thought to herself, rising slowly; she did not even come close to the top of his head.

They never disconnected their eye contact the whole time, reaching her hand out, bowing her head in respect as she would with any God.

He moved into her and smelled her hair, touching his cheek to her cheek.

Another wolf moved towards her, almost as big as the first one, grey in colour with a long black stripe down his back. Fiadh realised Con-ri and Cuan were standing before her, and she shivered in awe. She knew they were there to protect her and keep the path clear ahead.

They moved off into the forest, and she followed them.

Conn moved out with the men he had chosen to begin the search for Fiadh. His mind was full of fear for her. Is she alive? He could only hope. Out of the corner of his eyes, he could see a great shadow floating above his head in the distant trees.

A raven called out and circled around, moving over their heads.

The wings were much wider than an average raven, blacker than the night, and he knew this was a sign.

He knew it was Morrigu coming to aid them in their search. He felt sure now Fiadh was safe with the Gods watching over them, and he ordered them to move out.

The men looked to what Conn had seen, and they felt confident in their quest to search for Fiadh once more.

Morrigu, although very vindictive to those who were disrespectful to her, was not a danger to them.

Morrigu sailed over their heads, watching them closely. She had great anger in her heart today as she watched the invaders attack her children. She knew Fiadh was safe under the protection of Con-ri and Cuan.

They were her greatest warriors of the forest, who would defend her to the death.

Cernunnos had called to her when he heard Fiadh's prayers. You dare not cross Cernunnos even though she was a great goddess. He was lord of warriors and was more vengeful than she.

Her worry was they may not be working alone, and this was a battle of not just the man but of the Gods as well.

The men snored loudly, mumbling in their sleep as Galdor watched over them and the fire. They had landed on these shores with orders to attack and kill any who got in their path until they had control of the land and its people. He leaned back on the boulder and stared up at the sky and stars.

The seas had been very stormy on their way to this savage land. He had lost two ships and one hundred men, but they were disposable.

No man, woman or child was more important than gaining wealth or power for him. *The people on this land were, at best, savages*, he thought to himself. They would easily scare and be ruled in a matter of days.

He laughed to himself, rubbing his beard, "Oh, they will kneel to me and the Goddess, or they will be slaughtered."

Either way, he would have his way with all here and take everything he wished. Carman is all-powerful, as are her sons, Dubh, Dother and Dian.

They wanted their revenge on these savages, and all they wanted was the power and riches that would come with it.

No one could hear his cruel, dark laugh full of malice and greed. He glanced at the leg now cooking on the fire they had built on the beach.

The leg still had some hair on it, and he could see two of the toes falling to the side as the rest of the skin cooked and charred.

Nothing like a good enemy for dinner, he thought to himself. It took a bit longer to cook, but it would be well done for the morning when the men woke. They would need full stomachs for the march ahead in the morning.

The scouts should be back by then to give him the best direction to locate any towns. He had already filled up on one of the arms, pinking his tooth where a bit of flesh hung.

His teeth were filed and sharpened like a predator. Leaning over to the bone with the last piece of flesh still hanging on it, he bit in and pulled it off, savouring it.

These savages did not taste half bad, and he leaned over and picked up his drink, taking a long, deep mouthful. He had been on watch for a few hours now. Raising his foot, he landed a large kick on the man curled up with his back to him.

"Gravor, wake up!" He shouted and kicked him harder.

A greasy, long-haired, skinny man rolled over, looking at him. "Your watch, you useless waste. I need my sleep." Gravor's eyes looked red, wide and cold, his face paler than the sand he lay on.

Mumbling under his breath some insult, he jumped to his feet. His clothes were dirty and wet. He moved towards the fire and smelled the food cooking there. With a greedy smile, he licked his lips. He thought the sooner, the better morning came so he could eat.

He laughed a little, thinking back to how this fisherman was out fishing for his dinner. Now, he was dinner.

Galdor soon drifted off into a deep sleep, with Gravor watching over them for the rest of the night.

Chapter 4

A great ship stood off the coast of Dun Briste. Magnificent masts standing as tall as the cliffs themselves. Darkened sails with bright red stripes floating high above them. The wood, black and thick with carvings on every line, illustration of great battles, death, destruction and fires burning across lands of green.

Surrounding it is a deep, thick fog, hiding it from anyone who may wander to the shore line.

A strong foreboding presence lingered aboard.

She glided across the deck, long silver robes blowing in the wind as she leered across to the land she once invaded unsuccessfully.

Her long black hair, with white streaks streaming through it, flowed down her back to her waist.

They believed she was dead, and her sons were banished forever.

How mistaken they are, she thought to herself as she smiled wickedly back at the green land stretched out ahead of her. Now there is no Ai mc Ollamain (God of poetry), Be Chuille (The white sorceress), Cridhinbheal (Satirist) or Lugh Laebach (Magician) to stop her sons this time.

She is no longer a mere witch but a Goddess; she laughed callously to herself.

Their children are to blame for the cruel acts upon her and her beautiful sons, and at last, she will have revenge.

She stroked her hands through her hair, eyes sparkling with excitement and deep malice as she felt a strong figure come up alongside, towering over her. Dother leaned on the side of the taffrail with a sneer on his dark face. His eyes were dark as night and as malicious as his mother's.

He slithered almost like a snake as he turned to her, speaking in a deep, vicious tone.

"You think Dubh and Dian are positioned inside the walls of Tiernan's castle?"

His smile shining at the prospect of the murder and chaos they would instill in the people of this land once again. His cheeks pointing out from his sharp & menacing face.

Carman turned to him, smiling satisfactorily and replied, "I am sure they are well slotted into Tiernan's castle and, after all these years, trusted within Tiernan's people." she smiled triumphantly.

Carman had been planning this for years, and no one was going to stand in her way.

They had killed her once on this land, not knowing they had given her the greatest gift of being reborn into her goddess form.

This had given her leave to locate and reunite with her sons, to begin the plan of revenge on the Children of her foes. She should be thanking them; she smiled to herself.

"I am Carman, goddess of death for these lands." She called out to the sea in front of her.

Tiernan heard shouting coming down the corridor outside his door towards the great hall.

"My king, my king," the voice grew louder as he heard the thump of feet running towards him. Tiernan urged Cillian to open the door and let them in. Cillian, a very tall young man, got up from the chair by the door and raised the latch.

The door swung open with five men carrying something wrapped up in cloth. Tiernan's eyes widened. His heart sank seeing the horror in their faces. They had found his daughter.

He rushed from his seat and moved over to them. Leaning down, he pulled back the tarp. His eyes widened in shock at the monstrous sight in front of him. Yet he felt so much relief and joy that it was not his Fiadh.

Looking at the other men, his eyes, for the first time, showed worry. He looked back to the remains in front of him and moved closer to inspect.

The flesh was nearly completely removed from the bone on the legs and arms. He had never seen anything like it before in all his years. Leaning in closer to the arm, he could make out that no animal had done this.

His face turned to one of revulsion when he realised this was human teeth. The flesh had been torn from the bone by someone's teeth!

He thought to himself, what savagery could this be? He knew the other men were watching him in complete horror.

But they had fear in their faces and eyes, and he must not allow them to lose their nerve in the face of such monsters coming.

He balanced his hand on the floor and raised himself to stand in front of them, looking strong, unshaken and composed. Speaking loud and clear without losing momentum in his voice.

"Cover this poor soul and begin his rite of passage immediately. Fergus dying like this is a true warrior and a hero to our people; we will be ready and destroy this enemy. No doubt he died trying to protect his people." He continued, "They are men, to be sure, however barbaric they may seem. They can be killed, and we shall be the ones who will kill them. They picked the wrong land to invade."

He stood tall and confident as the men cheered in chorus. "We will kill them." The fear in their eyes and faces had subsided, and he knew he had regained their trust and their courage returned.

They carried the unfortunate soul's body out of the hall to be prepared for his family to say their goodbyes.

Tiernan's mind was racing with the new revelations brought to him: men eating other men.

This was a different kind of evil, one which he needed to name so he could fight it.

Fiadh moved fast behind her two great protectors. She still was in disbelief at what was in front of her as she watched their giant figures lead her through the forest to what she knew would be safety.

She could hear the trickling of water in the distance, her throat aching for the tenderness of moisture to quench her unbearable thirst.

The trees around her hummed in the wind loudly, and the night seemed to be drawing ever close again.

She exhaled loudly, releasing all the worry, feeling like she could finally relax. They came to an opening in a great tree whose branches seemed to reach beyond the others into the sky above.

It sparkled almost like the stars at night. She had investigated every corner of the forests around their land, and yet this tree she had never seen before.

Following Con-Ri and Cuan through the tree hollow, she glanced up, looking deep inside its great body, but she could only see darkness above.

It stretched far in front of her, and she knew this was no ordinary Oak tree but one of magic.

She felt tingles along her skin as her hair stood on end all over her body.

As she moved further inside, the water became louder and louder as she came out the other side to sunlight. But that was impossible, she thought to herself, its dusk?

She gasped at what she could see: a great valley and trees stretched either side as far as the eye could see, with mountains towering high in the distance.

A great waterfall dropped on either side of a big ravine. Its beauty was beyond anything she had ever encountered. The colours of the green leaves shimmered in the sunlight with gold and yellow flecks. A stream flowed in front of her. Kneeling down and cupping her hands, she scooped up the water and drank. It had a deep, brilliant blue colour, whispering to her almost in melody.

She splashed herself and felt instantly refreshed. Her face reflected on the water as the ripple dispersed, and she looked at herself for a minute.

Her big dark blue eyes looked tired, and her hair looked frazzled and tangled. She closed her eyes, soaking up the heat from the sun above and enjoying it. Birds flew around singing happily, and deer drank from the stream further up. Placing her feet in the water, she washed her legs and her arms, feeling the pain alleviate instantly.

This valley was truly of the Gods and enchanted, she thought to herself. Stroking her long brown hair with her fingers, she tried to remove the brambles and tangles from it. She thought of her father and how worried he would be, two days since she was gone. She could only pray the gods were protecting him and her people.

Her thoughts fell to Conn, how she would give anything to see his brilliant, warm smile now.

His gentle blue eyes that always fell on her with somewhat dismay but tenderness even when she had done something as stupid as going into the forest alone. How he would smile that bold, playful smile when he was teasing her. His strong, powerful arms always made her feel so small and safe when he was around. She cradled her arms around herself, longing to feel the comfort of his arms.

He would be searching for her, and no one would get in his way to get her back safe.

She lay her head on the grass. It felt so soft, staring up into the blue clear skies with the warmth of the sun lulling her as she drifted into a deep sleep without knowing.

Conn placed his sword into the ground and rose from his crouched position after giving Rian orders for the search. All the men looked at each other and nodded in understanding. These were no ordinary invaders and were here to kill them.

No mercy for them and no prisoners would be taken. They must find Fiadh safe. She was loved by all and was to be a leader alongside Conn one day. They need to protect the lineage of their people.

Conn spoke again, "You take the northern side, and we will take the southern side. May Cernunnos and Morrigu protect us and guide us."

Conn threw his sword over his shoulder, and Rian slapped his hand to his back as they separated.

Rian lifted the sap from the tree near him and brushed it through his blond hair to hold it back from his face. His eyes were as green as the grass they stood on. He was known for putting fear in any man who came to swords with him. The other men followed what Rian was doing. They placed their swords over their shoulders as he led them away from Conn.

Conn turned to Finian, his most trusted friend. "Finian, we must be alert at all times." Finian nodded and brushed his almost white hair away from his face. They had been friends since they were children. They fought fiercely and victoriously many times alongside each other.

They hadn't been born into a life of wealth and only mere farmers' children until the day Conn's family had been murdered and he was found fighting them by Tiernan. He took him under his care and treated him like his own kin. Conn rose fast and became a loved warrior and son to the Chieftain and the people.

Conn searched the sky above, looking for their guide. It had become darker as the great black clouds rolled in from the distance. Through the trees, he could see her wings blot out the light of the remaining glare of the sun from his eyes. She called out to him from above and started to move south. He looked back to his men, nodding to follow her.

Conn looked again to the skies above, knowing a great storm was coming. They would have to be careful now not to leave any tracks for their enemy to follow. He only hoped that Fiadh was safe and the gods would protect her.

He sighed deep in himself, trying not to show the worry on his face. His men needed him to show strength and confidence right now.

He could see her beautiful blue eyes in his thoughts, almost as blue as the sea surrounding their great land that he felt like he could drown in happily. Her infectious laugh was like a sweet melody caressing his ears, and her smile was kind that made his heart jump whenever she chose to give it to just him. He knew she would be okay, and he straightened his stature and determinedly pushed on.

Chapter 5

Tiernan leaned over to Aodh, his oldest advisor and friend, whispering so no one else could hear, "They found that poor unfortunate man's body behind our walls, Aodh."

Aodh's eyes widened as his pupils dilated in horror. He looked at his friend's bearded face and nodded with understanding that he had heard what was said. He was older and wiser than Tiernan but was a good soul yet fierce and strong when he needed to be. Aodh spoke low and with rage in his voice. "You mean we already have one of these demons amongst our people?"

Tiernan replied. "Maybe more!" Aodh expressed disgust at the words and pulled at his beard, deep in thought.

Tiernan spoke again, "Aodh, get your closest men to start searching the people for anyone who looks out of place." He continued, "This may narrow down where we can locate the enemy, tell them to travel in pairs and to watch their backs."

Aodh replied, "Tiernan, it's getting dark now. A storm is coming, and people will be turning in for the night." He continued, "We should call a curfew order so that only our trusted men are patrolling the grounds."

Tiernan nodded in agreement. "Give the order; may the Gods protect us and show us light on our enemies." Aodh bowed to his friend and left to carry out the orders. He stroked his long brown hair and felt a shiver run through his spine.

Tiernan sat down on his chair and stared up at the night sky through the window across from him. He noticed the storm coming in earlier and had hoped it would pass as it had done many times. This night, he feared, would not pass and would be a dangerous night for all out in the forests, including Fiadh and Conn.

He recalled the fierce young man he had brought home to his family all those years ago.

He thought back to the first time he had laid eyes on this young farm boy. His wild eyes burning with ferocity, he had only seen once in a warrior before.

He was swinging a sword at five men who were taunting him about the murder of his parents.

He had been one of the only survivors and had cut down eight men alone. At such a young age, he showed strength and bravery in such devastating circumstances.

Tiernan had arrived too late to save most of the people, but he would make sure this young man wanted for nothing. He took him into his own home with his family. His wife and daughter took to him without any questions. Fiadh grew close to Conn quickly, and she shadowed him everywhere he went.

Conn did not pay any attention to her for the most part and just let her follow him and watch him train. She soon picked up her own sword, and Conn himself started to train her. Their friendship grew every day in front of him. He watched their love for each other grow in front of him. He knew Conn and Fiadh one day would marry and make great leaders of their tribes.

He sent one of his best fighters away to find his daughter so if anything happened to him, they would hopefully be together and safe.

It was the best strategy for the future of our people, he thought to himself.

After much thought, he stood up from his seated position and moved out of the great hall down the quiet corridors, where only the guards stood and nodded as he passed.

He stepped out into the yard in front of the castle and glanced around at the people rushing into their shelters and houses built by the men for them. His eyes burned on every face, trying to pick out anyone that showed even the slightest bit of treachery.

No one stood out, and this was a problem. The enemy was amongst them and well hidden. All these faces were familiar, and he was sure to be loyal to their land and people.

He brushed his hands through his hair and sighed. How he wished their people could go back to feeling safe again. This wasn't the first time in his day that invaders thought they could destroy his home and people. They did not succeed last time, and he was determined not to let it happen now.

He walked back towards the hall and summoned Cillian. Cillian sprinted over to Tiernan when he called, bowing ever so slightly. Tiernan placed his hand on the young man's shoulder.

"Please go get Mc Ulcin; I need his wisdom right away." Cillian bowed again, disappearing as fast as he appeared. He was a runner, a scout and was able to move unseen anywhere.

Mc Ulcin lived in the forest nearby as he did not like living around people. He preferred to be at one with the land.

Tiernan moved back towards the hall as he shouted across the yard. "Bring me some food and water, Alanna, please. I must keep up my strength."

Watching her move quickly across the corridor, her long brown hair dancing on her shoulders as she moved swiftly and elegantly. He admired her for a moment and returned to the hall, sitting down in front of the fire burning there.

He knew dark days were ahead of them. Danger was hiding in the shadows of their home, and he worried how they would attack next. He only hoped it was just a he and not they.

He pondered for a minute, glancing at the door as Alanna gracefully entered with a tray of food for him. She smiled, her eyes showing concern.

He gestured to her to sit and join him. Alanna took his invitation and placed the food on the table before taking the seat next to him. She looked again at him with worried, soft eyes. He placed his hand over hers in reassurance and squeezed.

He never showed his softer side to anyone except Alanna and Fiadh since his wife, Fiadh's mother, had died many years ago. Alanna had watched over Fiadh and Tiernan like a Mother since that day he lost Aoife. She was, as her name meant, beautiful and joyful every day. She lit up every dark day with her presence, and the day he lost her, only Fiadh and Conn had given him reason to live on.

No other would ever replace her for him. Alanna was special to him in different ways, and he had grown to love her. He knew Aoife would approve of Alanna, and he smiled warmly at her.

He could not think of this now, and he removed his hand and ate what Alanna had placed in front of him. As Alanna was about to speak, the door burst open, and Cillian came racing in with a tall, thin, white-haired man behind him.

Tiernan stood up and crossed the room to greet the older man with a friendly smile.

"Mc Ulcin, thank you for coming so quickly." Tiernan gestured to him to take a seat, sitting next to him, calling to Alanna. "Please bring Mc Ulcin some broth to warm him up from the cold." Smiling softly, Alanna nodded before taking her leave.

Tiernan spoke quietly, "Mc Ulcin, we have grave danger in our midst, and I fear some may have infiltrated our walls already."

Mc Ulcin nodded as he wiped his face with his hand full of despair and looked up with his blood shot eyes before replying. "Tiernan, I have seen what has come to pass; a great evil is coming to destroy our lands." He continued, "I would have come sooner, but I don't walk so well any more. I was relieved you sent Cillian to retrieve me."

Tiernan leaned into Mc Ulcin's. "Tell me all that you have seen and what we must do." Mc Ulcin nodded to Tiernan to take a seat when Alanna came back with the broth. He looked up to her with his wrinkly smile, thanking her before he took the bowl in his shaking hands and had a long drink, sighing satisfactorily at its taste. "I needed that. It will warm my thoughts and my old bones."

Tiernan waited patiently as the old man settled before he began to tell what he knew.

When Mc Ulcin finished his premonition of what was to come, Tiernan's face had turned as white as the snow on Bencorr.

Alanna stood rooted to the spot at the realisation of what was to befall their people.

Cillian stared in horror. He had heard the stories since he was a child of the witch Carman. His mother had used this to keep him from disobeying her.

Tiernan, seeing the panic around him, cleared his throat again, taking the stance of the man that he is, confident and staunch in everything, before speaking. "Thank you, Mc Ulcin. Now we know what we are up against. We know what to look for." He continued, "You will stay within the castle walls for safety and to be my advisor." Mc Ulcin nodded in agreement and continued to drink his broth.

Impatiently, Tiernan waited for Mc Ulcin to drink more of his broth and regain his strength to tell what he knew.

It didn't take long before Mc Ulcin recited the horrors of days long gone of Carman, the witch from a faraway land who travelled with her three sons and caused chaos and death all around her.

He described her lust for destruction on all who didn't bow before her and her bloodthirsty sons. He spoke of the Tuatha de Danann, who finally captured and expelled Carman's sons from their land, locking Carman away where she died from hunger. Tiernan could hardly believe what he was hearing.

Mc Ulcin continued to tell of what he saw in his dreams. Carman now no longer was a witch, she had been reborn into a goddess form of the blood and death that she had brought on all around her.

"She has returned to gain her revenge on us all."

He wiped his brow and drank some more of his broth as Tiernan processed what he had just heard. The story was a mere myth passed down through the generations.

Tiernan had been told about Carman when he was growing up. She brought chaos to their lands, and his face grew worried. Tiernan rose from his seated position before speaking to Cillian. "Cillian, you speak nothing of what you have heard here. We don't want panic among the people." He placed his hand on Cillian's shoulder, looking intensely, waiting for his reply. "I understand Tiernan."

Tiernan smiled warmly, patting Cillian on the back before replying. "Cillian, bring Aodh, Gannon and Fallon to me. We must alert them about this new information. Arm yourselves and return with them," Cillian nodded proudly, leaving quickly to carry out his orders.

Chapter 6

The darkness had grown around Conn and his men. The wind had picked up, with a sharp mist rolling in around them. The air grew damp and cold. They could not light a fire tonight. It was too dangerous. Moving into a clump of trees, they all huddled together under their covers to keep warm.

Conn's mind wandered to Fiadh's face, her pearl white skin, her lips red as the berries on a mountain ash tree, her deep blue eyes that sent shivers through his very soul every time she looked at him.

He smiled warmly, thinking of the minute he would have her back under his care and love.

His anger rose from nowhere as he considered how he would scold her for going out alone in the forest again. The danger she brought on herself and others in her haste to always throw caution to the wind. He sighed deeply; he knew that only in a fleeting moment he would be angry, and then the relief of seeing her safe and alive would be all he would be able to show when he saw her.

Slowly, Conn fell into a deep sleep. He grew warmer and more at ease as gold light began to surround him.

It grew brighter and brighter as he squinted, trying to adjust to its brilliance. His eyes slowly could make out shapes as they began to form.

A great valley stretched out before him, Vast green forests reaching above on either side of the majestic mountains as far as his eyes could see. The trees lush and full of leaves of green and blue hue, unlike what he slept under.

He had never seen such beauty even on their land as this. A great waterfall was towering over the side of the mountain, water rushing down with a sound like thunder as its spray bounced through the air. He heard a voice murmur from a distance, and he followed its sound slowly with caution. There was a familiarity in it as he moved closer to its location.

He stood frozen to the spot as he realised the voices he could hear were that of his mother and father; their figures danced around each other and smiled. This can't be real; I'm in a dream. He shook his head and looked again.

They looked in his direction, moving towards him in a graceful, almost flying movement. His mother's long blond hair flowing behind her like gold sparking in the sun, her eyes shining, showing her smile warm with great happiness to see him.

His father moved beside her, looking as strong as the day he died. His long brown hair tied back off his face, and his beard gone. He looked younger than his years.

They descended upon him with delight as they said his name in unison, wrapping their arms around him tightly and squeezing. "My son, you have grown into a fine young man." His father looked at his face and stood back to take a good look at him. His mother placed tender kisses on his face and forehead as she held her arms around him, not wanting to let go.

Conn stood in shock as he knew this was a dream, but it felt real. How is this even possible?

His mind was racing. "I must have drunk something poisonous or ate something that is causing me to go mad."

As if his mother read his mind, she spoke softly, "This is real Conn, my beautiful son. We have been given a few moments to help you on your way to find Fiadh. This also gives us a chance to show you we are okay and together, watching over you every day."

His father then placed his hand on his shoulders. "We cannot stay, but we want you to search in your heart for Fiadh. Don't follow the usual routes or tracking. It will lead in the wrong direction. Feel your way to her as she will to you, my son." He continued, "There is a great danger ahead of you both which will not stop until you are parted forever, and they will destroy all that is of our beautiful land. Only you and Fiadh can stop this together."

Conn finally found the words to speak. "Mother, Father, I missed you," and he hugged them tight to him. They embraced him tightly back.

He already could feel them fading away. His heart ached, knowing they were leaving him again. His mother placed a hand on his cheek and whispered, "Look by the stream. We love you."

As they faded away and disappeared.

Conn felt the loss all over again, as he had the day they were murdered in front of him, and he ached as though a thousand knives had been jabbed into his heart. He placed his hands over his face, holding back the overwhelming sorrow he felt. "It's just a dream." He shook himself, trying to wake. "Wake up," he started to shout out, "wake up."

As he removed his hands from his face, he saw the stream ahead. Remembering his mother's words, he moved towards it.

The stream was bluer than any water he had ever seen. The water danced against the rocks within, yet no noise could be heard, how odd he thought to himself. As he moved closer, he could see a tiny figure on the other side laying down.

He could see the long brown hair falling around her back, and he instantly knew it was Fiadh.

His heart raced as he started to run towards her. "Fiadh," he called out. "Fiadh," he called out louder again. His heart was full of joy and relief. She lifted her head, turning to look at him, and her smile lit up to see him.

She jumped up from the ground and started running towards him, calling out his name with so much happiness. He could see the tears begin to fill her eyes as he swept her into his arms and pulled her tight into him. He kissed her head and her face, falling to her lips. She whispered breathlessly, "I know you will find me." Conn jumped as he felt someone shake him.

He opened his eyes to a whisper, "Conn."

Chapter 7

Conn's eyes opened to Finian leaning down beside him. The rain had begun pouring down, soaking everything around them, and Finian looked worried. "Conn, we have people moving in the trees to the east of us." He glanced over his shoulder.

Conn slowly moved his head and eyes in the direction Finian nodded in. He could see the shapes moving, although somewhat of a distance away from them. Their bodies were almost like only shadows as they moved swiftly, making no noise, gliding through the forest. *Were they tracking them?* He thought to himself.

Finian watched them move with caution, his eyes wide with discomfort. No one spoke; they just watched as these men moved along their land with the intent of killing them or anyone they came across.

Conn raised his hand in a gesture. All knew what he meant. They were going to take these invaders down now.

They each braced their swords, moving in synchronicity with Conn. They moved quietly behind the shadows through the trees, following them into a small clearing in the forest.

Everything had become deathly silent. Not even the rain was making a sound hitting the trees surrounding them.

Every droplet fell in almost a slow motion-like action as if time had stood still. The rain drops flicked off Conn's eyelashes down his cheeks onto his lips. His tongue flicked out, and he licked it off as his pupils dilated, his eyes looking wild and fierce.

They quickly moved in, howling as the shadowed faces came into focus, showing their shock at the appearance of Conn and his men.

Conn stalked forward with his sword raised, lashing out. Finian is right by his side, raising his sword with one swift swing, taking out the first man in front of him. The darkness only showed their eyes fierce in the night, swords sparkling as the rain lashed down hard on them as they swung at the enemies. The gargling cries from the invaders rang out one by one as they fell under Conn and his men's prowess.

Conn's sword cut hard and swift into the next man lunging towards him. He brought his sword down hard and fast, slashing into the man's neck as the blood spurted everywhere. He fell with a loud scream.

As the last one fell, Conn held his hand up in a hold position, standing over the bodies.

His eyes lit like fire as he nodded to each man and checked that none of his had fallen.

The rain trailed down his face as he breathed heavily, staring down now at the bodies lying in front of them. He leaned down to take a closer look. He noticed this one's teeth were filed into pointy-like shapes. Finian and the others looked at the other men's teeth, acknowledging all their teeth were the same. They stood in silence; only their heavy breathing could be heard, with the rain pouring hard down around them, smashing off the trees, washing the blood stains from their faces as the realisation settled in. These enemies were no ordinary invaders.

Conn felt the cold run through him at that moment, knowing they were facing a dangerous foe whom they had yet to know. These are only the foot soldiers sent in for the fun kill.

"Gather the bushes and sticks. Cover them up," Conn ordered his men.

They scattered in different directions to carry out his orders. He stared down at the torch one of the enemies had been carrying, still lighting as it lay by the redness of death flowing along the cracks in the ground, and he stood on it abruptly, extinguishing it and all signs of them ever being here.

Finian moved closer to Conn, looking down at the bodies with a worried look.

"They are like no others I have ever seen," Conn nodded in agreement before responding. "They are just men, Finian, they die! It's why they are here and who brought them. That is what we need to find out."

Conn called to his men, "Let's move out. No time to rest any more."

They gathered their gear and moved out into the oncoming orange hue, beginning to fall through the trees as the sun began to rise in front of them.

Conn took a breath, feeling a pull away from Dun Briste cliffs. He thought back to his father's words, almost hearing his voice in his ears. "Feel your way to her." Conn stepped forward, signalling to his men to follow him.

He was now going on his feelings to help him find Fiadh. He straightened his muscular frame, feeling more confident than previously, sure now Fiadh was safe.

Dubh reached across to his brother Dian, shaking him out of his deep sleep. Dian rolled over, his eyes widening as he growled low at his brother. "Why are you waking me, Dubh? It's not morning yet." He snarled at him.

Dubh put his finger to his lips to silence his brother and pointed to the door.

Dian could hear the movement outside and sat up abruptly, leaning over and grabbing his sword.

The room was dark except for the fire burning in the pit nearby.

The flicker of the flame shone up the side, showing their shadows fall against the back wall of their shelter.

Outside, they could hear many footsteps approaching, stopping across the way, shuffling as they moved what sounded like door to door. Muffled voices were getting closer to them.

Dian's dark eyes shot to his brother, his face thin and pale, lit by the fire. Dubh shifted slowly to his feet in preparation.

His thoughts had turned to the possibility they had been found out. "That's impossible; they think we are sons of the old farmer and have been here for years," he whispered to Dian as if he could hear what he was thinking.

Dian nodded in agreement, but his heart thundered in his chest at the prospect of having to fight their way out of here. He was ready as he grasped the handle of his sword.

The feet stopped at their door as the loud banging echoed around the room. Dubh moved fast towards it and swung it open.

The three men standing at the door had swords drawn at ready. Dubh spoke clearly and confidently with a look of confusion on his face.

"What is wrong? Are we under attack?"

One of the three men stepped forward, replying, "No, we are just checking the homes to make sure everyone is secure and safe."

Dubh spoke up again, "With drawn swords, with women and children behind some doors. Are you trying to put fear in our people so they can't sleep?"

The men glanced at each other, looking embarrassed and put up their swords out of view.

The tallest of the three men apologised before bidding them a peaceful night, retreating back down the street, followed by the other two men.

Dubh smiled smugly at his brother and whispered, "They will never see us coming so gullible."

Dian laughed, running his hand through his greasy, long hair, replying, "We must put our plan of action in motion behind these walls." Dubh nodded in agreement. "We will start by poisoning the water of the guard, lowering their watch." Dian continued as he closed the door, feeling confident in their plan of attack.

Rian and his men dodged in between the trees one by one, avoiding detection. They had been searching for any clues as to the whereabouts of Fiadh when they happened upon the invaders coming from the boats. They watched as creatures also rose from the sea in their thousands.

Rian knew this was no fight they could win with the mere handful of men he had in his company. His best defence was in detecting weakness, observing and relaying all information back to Tiernan.

It had just become a new mission for him and his companions.

The men watched in shock at the lines of otherworldly creatures marching onto their land.

They were horrified at the ghastly sights they were seeing. They looked to Rian for his words.

He quickly composed himself and placed his hand on Connors's shoulder, "Run like the wind back to Tiernan and relay what we have seen here. Don't stop for anything, and stay behind the trees at all times. They must know what is coming before it is too late."

Connor nodded in agreement and took to his heels without another word needing spoken.

Rian turned to the other men and spoke. "We must blend in and watch them every step of the way." He began to remove his outer garments and reached for more sap off the trees as he rubbed it all over him.

He then reached for the mud surrounding him, painting his face and all over his body. The men followed suit, and soon, you could only see the whites of their eyes.

The air had become musty with a stench of evil all around them.

Chapter 8

Fiadh woke with a start from the dream she had of Conn. She felt sure that was not just a dream, and he had seen her, too. She stretched, running her fingers through her hair. Leaning to the stream, she cupped her hands and drank the fresh, clear water.

She sensed something behind her and slowly rose from her kneeling position, turning to find a giant Stag standing before her.

His antlers stood tall on his head like the branches on the great Ash tree in the forest by her home. His regal form towered over her, taller than any Stag she had ever seen. She knew this was one of the many forms of Cernunnos right away, and she bowed low in front of him. In an instant, a hand was placed on her shoulder, and Fiadh jumped with surprise.

Standing before her was no longer a Stag. It was a very beautiful man with golden hair smiling softly at her. His eyes shone brightly down on her, a deep, warm emerald green. He slowly took her hand and ushered her to rise from her kneeling position.

His voice was strong and full of power as he spoke to her.

"Fiadh, welcome to the Island of Souls." Fiadh's eyes widened, and understood now where she was.

She began to panic, wondering if she had passed over. As though he could hear her thoughts, he spoke again.

"No, Fiadh, you are still with the land of the living; you are under the protection of your ancestors, and we can transfer one person every seven years onto the Island." He continued, "The only other way for any living person to visit is during time of rest."

She knew now Conn had been there with her, even if it was just in his dreams.

Cernunnos looked into her eyes, showing concern as he began to explain who the invaders were.

He was all too familiar with Carman and her sons.

As he explained the details behind the previous encounter with Carman and her sons, Fiadh realised the seriousness of the danger they brought.

Cernunnos explained that Carman would be a serious threat as she no longer lived in a human form. He could not tell her if they would be successful in their battle.

Cuan and Con-ri moved up by his side as he continued speaking, "Carman is one of the greatest evils our land has come up against, and this time, she returns with her sons and allies who have no value on life."

"I believe they are the Fomorians; all they know is death, leaving decay in their wake. They have no links to love or family. They don't want to die. However, they have no fear of death. Unlike you and your people, they can use these emotions against you. This is also your greatest strength, love and loyalty to each other and your people. It is the greatest link in all plains, spiritual and living. They once lived on this land, vicious, without any compassion for anything. They can look like a man, but many look like demons."

Fiadh felt nervous about what was to come. She exhaled before speaking. "What must we do to beat such powerful enemies?"

Cernunnos looked to Con-ri and Cuan, placing his hands on their mighty backs as he replied, "You and Conn must travel to Ui Breasail, the land off the coast that appears but once every seven years and bring back assistance from the Tuatha De Danann. The only way to get there is through Bru na Boinne."

"Morrigu is already with Conn, guiding him to where you will come together again. She is but one of the nine Gods that once helped the four thwart Carman's previous attempt at taking over our land." He continued, "There is no earthly manner to destroy Carman on this occasion. Only they can help you."

"Cuan and Con-ri will protect you until you are safe with Conn again. They will return to me until the time is right for their strength and power to be used in the greatest battle these lands have seen. Now eat for strength, my child," as he pointed to a table with berries, and what she could smell was a warm broth that smelled just like what her mother used to make for her.

Fiadh nodded in understanding, thanking Cernunnos for his assistance and protection.

As she walked to the table and glanced back to speak once more with Cernunnos, he was nowhere to be seen.

She sat on a stone chair so enormous her small legs dangled off, not reaching the ground. It had great carvings on the back and arms of what she recognised as the mighty wolves by her side and the great Stag that was Cernunnos.

It appeared to have a story written in the carvings.

It showed a battle with creatures bearing jagged teeth and deformed faces. She wondered if these were the Fomorians he spoke of.

She shuddered as if someone had walked across her soul, and she ached to be with her family, to go back to the days previous when all was well in their land. Fiadh ate the food laid out for her, knowing she must gain her strength for what was to come.

Tiernan had fallen asleep sitting up in his chair, woken by a door slamming further down the hall. He leapt up, drawing his sword, and Cillian jumped to attention along with the other men in the room. Footsteps came racing down the hall, and the door flung open.

Gannon appeared at the door looking dishevelled, gasping the words out.

"The men are dropping on the walls for no reason. A great ship has been spotted coming out of the mist on the coast by Dun Briste, and many boats have landed on the beach. Connor has returned with the information."

Tiernan knew as quickly as this word had travelled that Carman and her men would have a head start and closer than they knew.

It was clear to him they had poisoned the guard and were planning ahead for the attack.

How could he identify the enemy when it could be one of their own people or someone who knew their ways and land well? Tiernan spoke up as the dawn hit the windows of the castle. "Wake all the men and stop them eating anything or drinking anything that came in contact with the night guard." Gannon and Cillian immediately raced out to carry out the orders.

Tiernan adjusted his sword onto his Leine and stood tall and sure again in front of the rest of the men as he gestured to them to follow him.

Connor sat huddled over with a cover around his shoulders; as Tiernan approached, he looked up at him with tired eyes.

"Tell me all, Connor." As he ushered him to his feet, supporting him with Aodh on the other side, helping him through the courtyard doors of the castle. Aodh rushed to a chair and pulled it over for Connor to sit.

Tiernan's voice was clear and calm as he questioned Connor's sudden arrival back from the search for Fiadh. Connor spoke of the great army they saw rise from the sea, along with the many boats coming to shore.

His voice grew hoarse as he began to speak of the woman atop a giant creature he could only describe as a beast of unimaginable horror.

Tiernan's eyes grew dark and angry at the revelations he had just heard.

He questioned Connor more about the number of invaders he had seen and how able they looked. Connor spoke clearer now. "There are many more than we are, Tiernan; we need the clans to come together to have any hope of victory."

Carman sat tall atop the Cresocia as she rode across the land towards Tiernan's Castle, feeling victory would be hers. The Cresocia was as frightening and dangerous as he looked. His great horns towering above her, his teeth protruding through his lips, almost covering his entire face. All that you could see was his huge eyes staring menacingly from behind. He was larger than any creature on this land but moved as quickly as the most agile.

She smirked and began to chant. "Rise the grey and the ungodly from the castaway depts of the seas, begin your return and revenge upon those who dare banish you from the soil you are made of!"

From the waves, a slow mist began to rise with an ear-piercing shrieking.

Their heads appeared first, balding grey. Their eyes black and soulless, their bodies misshapen as they crawled slowly onto the white sands. Their faces disfigured and unsightly as they began to stretch out from their crawling positions to stand on two legs. They had not used their legs after living in the sea for such a long time. Their feet had webbed, their bodies had boils growing on them.

She smiled as she watched her legions rise from the depths, knowing she had them to assist her revenge on the children of the Tuatha De Danann.

They would move fast towards their destination, and soon, she would make them all beg for their lives. *Would she let them live?* She cackled to herself.

"Maybe, maybe not," Dother looked at his mother with a malicious scowl, knowing her very thoughts without her having to speak them.

She glanced around the land that had caused her death and separated her from her beautiful sons many years ago. She thought of the cruelty she intended to disperse on the people of this land and stroked her hand through her hair, waving her arm, ordering them to move faster.

Galdor looked up to Carman and cheered in unison with the Formorians around him. The time had come to fight and destroy.

Goll stood back and watched over his Fomorian Kin as they marched under the banner of Carman the witch. His face sunken, his skin greying from the long life living in the darkest of the depths of the sea. His eyes protruded like that of a frog and stung with the bright light from the day around him.

He waited many years for this chance to take over the land again and bring chaos and destruction to the children of those who had banished him and his ilk. He stretched out his scrawny arm to block the now-rising sun from his eyes and smirked up towards Carman. She is but a means to get what I want, he thought, and then she will be of no use.

He remembered the days when Fomorians ruled this land, and all humans were slaves to their will.

Until some Fomorians mixed with the Tuatha de Danann, betraying all of them and giving the humans leave to exile them to the Sea.

He growled low under his breath so as Carman would not hear or suspect anything was not as it seemed.

He was the leader of the Fomorians but did not let on there was any.

It was better for them that Carman believed they were just mindless creatures under her power. He intended this land to be his, to stand on the people who blocked the way of that coming to be.

Chapter 9

The people were beginning to whisper amongst each other as they realised that all was not well in their land. The fear had taken on a life of its own, and they needed wisdom and support from those who had the knowledge and power to give them the comfort they had known.

Tiernan knew this as he strode out into the yard and the coming dawn of awakenings for him and his people. The sky had an eerie white hue stretching out above them as far as the eye could see. The wind howled unbearably around them, with a warning being whispered in his ear as to what was coming. There was no way to make this danger any lighter for them.

He looked as strong and resolute as always as he moved in front of the many worried eyes of Mothers and children; he knew they would be in need of his reassurances. He had none for them, and all great leaders will always tell them the truth. He stood tall as he began to speak.

The silence grew around him as everyone held their breaths for what he was going to divulge.

"My family, my friends, it is with great sadness I must tell you of a great menace that has landed upon our shores. They have already begun a savage attack across many towns with no remorse." Loud gasps came from the women staring up at him in the realisation that their feelings were being verified.

Tiernan paused before continuing, "Know that we are strong as a people, and I will protect you from outside forces with my own life. We will prevail over this threat that attempts to harm us. They will never remove the power we have together. We are the clay of this land. Our blood runs through the very soil we walk on, as did our people before us. The spirits are on our side; we just need to stay alert and aware of the threat so they do not catch us off guard."

The crowd gathered tightly, placing their hands on one another's shoulders, standing strong with the fear gone from their eyes and replaced with love and strength. Tiernan turned to Aodh and Cillian before speaking softly. "You all will take the underground tunnels and travel to Ben Gorm for safety with the Children. Aodh, Cillian, you will lead them there."

Tiernan spoke low as his eyes traced the faces all around him in the background, searching for the enemy they had within. They could be any of the people that came in looking for protection.

He knew they also could have been in their company for years and waiting for the moment to strike. His eyes followed a line of men and women with children waiting for the new batch of food which Aodh's wife and Alanna had brewed up under the watchful eye of their guards so no treachery would befall them again. He had lost thirteen men on the wall due to some poisoning, and he wasn't going to let that happen again.

Tiernan nodded to Aodh and Cillian to begin the evacuation of the vulnerable. He knew they had a long, treacherous journey; however, Ben Gorm Mountains were very high and hard to get to when you're not aware of the hidden opening.

The passages would give them part of the journey below land and far away from where Carman had landed. He was taking a chance on the foe not being amongst the people he was sending there, but he felt sure they were not and would be staying close to him.

He stood tall and called to the people, "In this time, we have a hostile force landed upon our shores. We will not be beaten, and we will bring you back as soon as we are victorious. I will not divulge where I am sending you, but you will be safe and under the guidance of Aodh, Cillian and some of our other men. The great goddess Eriu will watch over you and guide you peacefully to the sanctuary." He continued, "These are dark times on our beautiful land, but we will prevail. Now follow Cillian, collect your things, travel light and quietly."

No one spoke as they all moved to follow Cillian, as Aodh and Tiernan whispered to each other. Aodh watched closely all around him as they stood shoulder to shoulder.

He could feel a weight of treachery near him, watching them closely, and his anger grew inside. Tiernan placed his hand on Aodh's arm as he narrowed his eyes and said, "I feel it also, my friend. They are here and watching. We must not let them see where you are going." Aodh nodded and moved towards Cillian.

Dubh and Dian stood close but not close enough to overhear what was being said. They knew Tiernan would be keeping his plans only to those within his circle of closet advisors and men. Had they dealt their hand too soon, with Tiernan now preparing for the onslaught and moving the people. The leverage they had was weakening already, and their mother would be furious with them.

Dian looked to Dubh as they contemplated what they could do to bring the advantage back to them. With no knowledge of Tiernan's direct plans, though, they were at a loss.

Dian moved closer to Tiernan as he tried to hear what was being said but was quickly blocked by four big men and shoved back towards Dubh. Aodh was moving the vulnerable outside of the walls, and Dian nor Dubh could see which direction they were travelling in.

They looked at each other with worry now, as they knew without the women and children, Tiernan would feel more at ease and more confident when in battle.

They watched as the last hems of the leine moved out of the gates and closed behind them.

"What must we do, Dian?" Dubh quickly turned to his brother and asked.

Dian scratched his dirty face in thought as he scanned the walls, looking for a way so that they may view the direction taken.

He scowled, "There is no opening I can see to the wall's brother," he continued. "Tiernan has foreseen this and covered all walls with only his most trusted. We have failed our first task, and I fear our mothers' wrath will not be merciful," as he remembered the last time he failed her and ran his finger along his all but faded scar, still feeling the sting of the hot sword penetrating his face hidden under the beard he had grown.

Dubh spoke low with a callous tone, "You have failed Dian, not I," he continued. "I warned you not to make such a premature poisoning of the wall, and you went ahead."

Dubh knew his mother would favour him over Dian as she always had, and he would not feel her wrath.

Dian's face dropped with disappointment, and he turned away so his brother could not see his thoughts. He wished he could just run from this family and not look back. He had tried this once before and failed.

His mind wandered back to the beautiful cliffs of Keiss, where he had found peace and love once after they were banished from this land many years ago. Colina, his mind wandered to the beautiful woman he had loved and lost to the wrath of his mother.

His heart ached, and he closed his eyes tight. There was no escaping his mother so long as their blood was connected. He was all but a slave to her will, and this was his prison.

Aodh took the lead as Cillian flanked to the right, watching eagerly around him as they moved through the forest at a steady pace. They had not far to go until they would come to the hidden passage. The Mothers hushed the children over and over as they followed.

Aodh looked around them into the forest with worried faces. Aodh held his hand up as he leaned down to a large boulder and began to push it with another man, revealing a small opening in the ground.

Turning to Cillian, Aodh ordered him to take the lead and ushered the people to follow. Cillian descended into the hole, feeling a small rope in his hands as he slid a few feet into the hidden passage. He stood waiting and assisting each person as they slid down behind him.

He strained his eyes into the tunnel around him. It was so dark you couldn't see two feet ahead of you beyond the light coming from the entrance above. He called out to them to move along the wall and wait until everyone was below.

The smell of earth and stagnant water tickled the senses around his nose, causing his eyes to leak somewhat. Aodh leaned into the opening, calling out, "All accounted for!"

He climbed down through the hole as he pulled the boulder back into place, covering the entrance and extinguishing all light from above.

No one spoke. All that could be heard was the shifting of feet and breathing. Aodh struck something again and again hard, making an echoing dull clanging sound as a great flash of light burst all around them, lighting everything.

Everyone placed their hands in front of their eyes, trying to adjust to the brilliant light that surrounded them.

They could clearly see now a long tunnel ahead that was narrow and damp. The roots from the trees and grass above poked out along the tunnel from the mud. There was great unease yet slight relief all around as they knew no one would find them down there. These passages were only known to the king and his closest confidants for this exact reason.

Aodh called out to Cillian to move out; he would take up the rear, and his son Cronan would fall into the centre.

Darkness was falling across the land again with the sense of an approaching storm in the air.

Tiernan strapped on his sword, calling to Fallon.

"We are moving out now, my friend." Fallon stood up immediately, calling out to each man as he crossed the courtyard.

Dubh and Dian looked up at Fallon in surprise.

They had not heard a word of the plans as to what would happen. Fallon glanced at them as they moved towards the rest of the men, and he called out. "Irial, Flann, not you two. I want you two to stay here." Dubh nodded, scowling as he turned to his brother and walked away. Fallon had never liked the brothers, and he didn't trust them from the day he met them. He would not want them with him when he needed someone to watch his back.

Dian whispered to Dubh with a slight growl in his tone, "What shall we do now, brother?"

Dubh hushed him with a scolding reply, "We wait till they are gone and move out to meet Mother to alert her of Tiernan's counteractions." Dian nodded in agreement as he watched through slitted eyes Tiernan and the rest of the men move out.

Chapter 10

Carman rode high and confident as they marched further into the countryside, the vast green stretching out before them. Her army of men and Fomorians is substantial and formidable. She smiled callously as she scoured her surroundings, searching for potential foe.

Night was drawing in slowly, the air of a storm on its way, tickling her skin. She shivered happily as she felt the taste of death within her grasp.

She spotted smoke further ahead coming from many areas and knew this was their first town to take. She licked her lips in excitement as she turned to Dother, pointing her slim, long finger in the town's direction.

His eyes had already seen the smoke floating up in the sky, and he rubbed his hands with wicked contemplation as he reached for his sword, calling out his orders. "We will move into the town and kill all that rebel against us."

Carman had no intention of stopping for such an insignificant target, she would allow her son and her men to enjoy some easy sport before the main event. She marched on without a second glance as Dother and over one hundred men split off and moved towards the smoke billowing out over the trees in the distance.

Her thoughts lingered always on her victory over Tiernan, to conquer and control all of this land.

She thought back to days when she had great power on this land, and they bowed to her as she passed. Those days would come again whether they wished for it or not.

Tiernan and Fallon marched ahead of their men into the forest. The oncoming storm would be a hindrance in this difficult time. However, Tiernan would use it to his advantage.

Fallon cleared his throat and spoke quietly.

"Tiernan, the direction Carman is coming from is passing one of the towns we have not evacuated; they have no idea what is coming their way." He continued, "They will be slaughtered, nothing more than insects under their feet."

Tiernan looked into Fallon's solemn eyes without worry. "I have already sent someone when Connor brought the news of the direction Carman was travelling to warn them of what danger was coming." Fallon's eyes widened with admiration yet again for this man who had earned his respect over the many years they had known each other.

They moved with quiet swiftness through the trees hidden from the track of the main road. They had left only a hundred men behind and given the order to evacuate should they need to.

Tiernan sent four more men to the surrounding clans to call for them to meet for what is sure to be war. Ruari from the west, Lugh from the east, Kyra's from the north will be the closest and fastest to arrive.

Fiachra was further south and would take longer to arrive. However, he had a strong force of great fighters behind him and would be a great asset if all did not go well.

Tiernan looked to the sky in silent thought, asking for strength and wisdom in these times of peril.

He knew there would be no killing Carman by any man's tool, but the army she had with her would bleed, and they would concentrate on victory over them.

Conn and his men moved fast through the trees, watching every movement around them. No one questioned Conn's change of direction. They followed, knowing he had his reasons. His heart pounded in his chest with determination, knowing he was not far from Fiadh. He knew the key was with her and him and whatever Cernunnos had planned.

Time was of importance, and he needed to be with her again.

Morrigu watched from above, making sure the path was clear. She knew Conn was on the right path, and soon they would be reunited. Two days of hard travel with small sleeps in between had been strenuous but necessary.

Already, the land was becoming rank with the foulness Carman had brought upon it. The trees looked dull, and the grass was greying; the air was stagnant.

Conn placed his hand in his leine, pulling out the pieces of yellow petals of the Gorse flower, and placed them in between his palms, rubbing them back and forth with vigorous movement.

He placed his fingers beneath his nose. The fragrance oozed through his senses, waking him up and bringing relief from the stench. Finian and the other men followed suit.

They could see an opening up ahead in the treeline. In the distance, a mound was appearing above the ground with the sun falling behind it, giving it a glorious glow of orange, making it seem like a dream. From where they were, it looked huge, but as they drew closer, its enormity became increasingly clear.

None of them had laid eyes on Bru na Boinne before, and their eyes grew wide with astonishment at all of its splendour. The grass upon it and surrounding it was Emerald green, the greenest they had ever beheld. There stood five statuesque trees around it in a perfect circle, with mighty branches stretching out over their heads that seemed to touch the very sky above.

The leaves were of what can only describe as a blue colour with gold shimmering off them. They felt a great calm as they walked under the cover of their majesty.

They knew they had crossed into a truly magical place, and they murmured to themselves as they glanced around, mesmerised.

In between each tree were other smaller mounds also in a ring-shaped effect with stones connecting to each end.

Conn noticed off to the right of them, one of the trees had a great opening in the trunk, and there appeared to be a glow from within. He called out to his men, "Sit down, rest now and eat; we have arrived at our destination for now."

He looked back to the tree with the opening and slowly moved towards it. There was a deep silence all around him, and the stench which had offended his nose previously was no more. It was replaced with a warm, sweet scent.

As he drew closer to the tree hollow, he could see shadows move in the backdrop of it. He stopped dead in his tracks, ready for attack. The shadows grew, two larger ones and one much smaller behind. The first two he could see now, and he stared in awe as the great wolves appeared, standing tall, taller than any wolf he had ever encountered.

His hair began to stand on end all over his arms and neck in anticipation.

Conn already knew that the figure trailing behind these two enormous creatures was who he had been searching for.

He moved forward at a quicker pace, paying no heed to the gigantic Wolves that lay in front of him.

His breath quickened, and his heart raced with a thundering rhythm inside him as she appeared from the hollow and her eyes gravitated towards him.

He gasped out loud as Fiadh's eyes met his, sending shivers through his very being.

Fiadh caught her breath as she realised this is no illusion and Conn is in front of her.

She smiled brightly, running to him as fast as she could, leaping into his outstretched arms. He inhaled her, running his fingers in her hair and closed his eyes to take in every piece of her. Fiadh melted into the strength of his body and the nurturing of his love.

She finally felt at ease and knew there is hope for victory in these chaotic times.

Conn slowly placed her little feet back onto the ground, grasping her chin in his hand as she looked up to him. His brilliant blue eyes stared into hers with intense devotion as Fiadh's face flushed a brilliant red.

He reached into the very depths of her heart and soul. No one could make her feel as he did. She only ever felt truly like a woman when she was with him. He grazed her lips sensually with his as he whispered, "My love, you look very happy to see me."

She could no longer hold back her tears, and she kissed him passionately in return.

Behind Conn, she could hear the hurried feet approaching as Finian and the other men called out. He spun around and raised his hand for them to be still. They now saw Fiadh, and they dropped to their knees as she approached. Fiadh beckoned them to stand and hugged Finian. He smiled in relief as the other men cheered in jubilation.

She laughed warmly as Conn wrapped his arm around her slim waist and cradled her close to him. He was not going to be leaving her side ever again, he thought to himself.

Galdor and Dother marched towards the village ahead with the devious intent of destruction. The Fomorians marched alongside them, snarling menacingly with their dark eyes fixated on their prize.

Galdor was excited for the many he could eat here in this little village, and he licked his lips, savouring the thought.

Anyone was easy pickings for him so long as they were not members of Tiernan's family. Carman had made it clear to him that if he touched anyone of importance, she would flay him alive and feed him to the Fomorians.

He wanted so much to try Tiernan's family, though they were taboo, which made it all the more tempting.

His eyes grew darker as the thoughts made his mouth water if one of them fell by accident, and he did not know they were members of Tiernan's lineage. He cackled to himself, knowing he would do as he pleased and Carman would be none the wiser.

He stilled his laugh as he felt Dother's eyes on him and watched him raise his eyebrow and hold his gaze with an unnerving warning in them.

Dother knew Galdor and his men were frivolous, and he would watch them carefully. While they are a means to an end for this endeavour, he is no fool and knew they could not be trusted.

Dother raised his hand, and all eyes turned to him as he spoke, "We will take this village with minimal death today."

The Fomorians mumbled under their breaths, unhappy with these new orders. Galdor sniffed, displeased with the obstacle to his plans, scowling in the direction of Gravor and his other men. Their eyes fell on him, also unhappy with this new order and felt they had been tricked.

Dother spoke loud with virility, "Do not test my mother's wrath nor mine."

Silence fell across the Fomorians and Galdor's men as they moved closer to the village.

They had nothing to worry about with these weak people who would be but mere fishermen, women and children.

As they moved in towards the village, their thirst for destruction grew. Dother raised his hand and gestured to Galdor to move in with his men.

They began to run at speed, yelling with a high-pitched screech that would send terror through any soul. Mud was hindering their pace as they sunk into the watery earth beneath their feet. The rain and wind had picked up with intensity and were pushing against their progress.

The people of the village hurriedly moved around the village in a panic. They had gotten the warning too late and now surrounded and had nowhere to go.

The head of the village, Cronan, moved through the crowd of panicked women and children, giving orders and directions to the able-bodied men.

They had hidden cavities under the village in the event of attack and no retreat. The scout ran up to Cronan, whispering that the enemy was only a short distance away, his eyes full of shock at what he had seen.

He spoke breathlessly, divulging his findings. "There are those who are not even human amongst them, Cronan."

Cronan placed his hand on his shoulder, replying, "They bleed. They die."

Smiling, slapping him on the shoulder, "Now go take up your weapon and prepare with the rest of the men." The women and children and older of the town moved out across the town and began to lower themselves into their hiding places.

The men hid from view and held their weapons nervously, their eyes darting to each corner of the village, ready to ambush them.

Cronan knew Tiernan was on his way with his men, and others would follow from each clan. He just hoped they would arrive on time to help.

Their little village had only thirty able-bodied men who were no match to a hundred or so monsters determined to kill them. That's when he heard the high-pitched shrieks coming towards them. It was time. He called out. "Fight hard. Tiernan will be with us soon."

Chapter 11

Tiernan moved quietly and swiftly, ever nearing Cronan's village. Their scouts came back advising them that Carman had broken off from the hundred or so men and Fomorians heading for the village. She had taken a path directly towards Tiernan's castle. She had not predicted this move by Tiernan, and he knew he had the upper hand here.

Dother held back as Galdor and the Fomorians raced into the village, screaming with ear-piercing screams. Cronan and his men leapt out to the oncoming invaders, slashing hard and knocking some to the ground. More and more Fomorians rushed them.

Galdor laughed loudly as he slashed the arm off one man and then his leg, speaking with an unmerciful, hateful tone. "You shall not die yet!" Dothur watched from the side-lines as the Fomorians rushed through the small village, taking down every man in their way.

Quickly, the village was overrun, and some men were disarmed and rounded up into the middle of the village. Galdor smiled as he dragged another man to the centre of the circle and licked his lips as he wiped some blood off the man's slashed face with his fingers.

Galdor moved his fingers to his mouth and flicked his tongue out like a snake, licked it with a hungry murmur.

He savoured the taste and looked into the horrified man's eyes before speaking, "Don't worry, I am not going to eat you. I have a taste I much rather try of richer blood."

Dother moved forward, his long black hair flowing down his back, his tall skinny body looking elegant and ominous. He spoke loud and controlled, no emotion of anger or hate, just bland with the promise of danger behind it. "Where are the women and children?" he was met with silence.

He spoke again, "If you do not tell me where they are, each of you will die a slow, excruciatingly painful death!"

Silence continued, and Gadlor snarled loudly. "Let me show them what we can do, and they will speak then." Dother raised his hand in denial at Galdor's request and raised his voice so loud it boomed across the village. "People of this village, come forward, or I will give leave for my men and the Fomorians to eat every one of these men alive, and then you and your children." You would not have thought such a frail, thin man would have such a powerful roar.

Cronan shuddered and stared into these monsters' faces with loathing. Out of the corner of his eye, he could see the first woman, his wife, climbing from her cavity hidden under the street with regret.

His heart sank as, one by one, the people climbed from their hiding places and began being gathered up by the Formorians. They were shoved and hit them, forcing them into a separate circle further down the village.

Dother grinned victoriously, shouting his orders at Galdor. "Kill the men, have at them whatever you wish;

women and children will go with me and some of the men to catch up with my mother." Cronan and the other men's faces grew in horror as they paled to hear their faith.

Galdor was not happy, he wanted to taste the flesh of the young, not these men.

Lush young meat he wanted to savour. His anger was growing at these new rules. He had been told all was for the taking.

He clenched his fists with a bubbling rage growing more and more inside.

Dother turned, giving his orders to move them out as the men of the village could only watch them go.

The Fomorians snarled in excitement as they had not eaten for an age the flesh of man. They relished the chance to taste the flesh of those who had banished them so many years ago from this land. Galdor had lost interest and stared on after Dother and the real prizes that he led away.

Tiernan and Fallon marched through the forest outside of Cronan's village. Tiernan called his orders out to the men to spread out and surround the village. Dusk was slowly moving in on them, and they would use it to their advantage.

Tiernan de robed himself quickly, gathering the sap off the trees around him.

He knelt down as he began his prayer, *"Valiant Nuada of the white sword, who subdued the Firbolg of blood, for the love of the tribe, for pains of Danu's children, Hold thy shield over us, protect us all."*

Slowly, a white mist began to form around his ankles, seeping up from the ground and swirling faster and faster, engulfing them.

A faint whispering surrounded them through the mist in an almost song. Tiernan knew that Nuada was watching over them.

He plunged his hands into the mud beneath his knees and covered himself head to toe until all that could be seen was his eyes full of fire and fury. They blended into the forest around them; all that could be seen was the white of their eyes, wild and ferocious.

Tiernan raised his arm as he did. Every man duplicated his action to pass on the order around the men. Soon, all arms were raised high, and they knew the order moving in, encircling the village.

They moved faster and faster under the cover of the forest before pausing at the outskirts. They could see figures standing over a circle of people all on the ground.

Tiernan could see Cronan's face under the glow of a torch-lit beside them and, to his horror, a man tied to a post with a leg and an arm missing. The Fomorians were laughing excitedly as they danced around, drinking and eating from what he could see was someone's leg.

Tiernan's anger grew, he wanted to scream and kill them all. What kind of savages are these creatures, he thought to himself.

Fallon moved in close to Tiernan after seeing what was happening in the village. "I can't see many of the people there and no women or children, Tiernan. What will we do?" he asked. "They must be hidden in one of the homes," he continued. That is dangerous. "If we attack, they will all be slaughtered."

Tiernan glanced over at Fallon before replying, "We have to go in no matter what we do. They are going to kill them anyway. This way, we can limit the dead." Fallon nodded in agreement and moved back to his position, awaiting the forward order.

Tiernan clenched his fist around his sword and shouted so that the closest men to him could hear him, and they, in turn, shouted the order so it could be passed around. Tiernan moved forward with haste and determination in his heart.

The Fomorians did not see them coming till it was too late as they rushed out from the surrounding forest with the mist swirling around them. The Fomorians and Galdor looked up to see the figures running from the forest, their eyes widened in shock.

A sea of whispers surrounded them, high-pitched and deafening to their ears. They looked like unearthly spirits floating towards them through a wall of fog.

Cronan and the other men jumped to their feet, taking advantage of the surprise attack, and lashed out at their captors. Tiernan swung his sword hard, taking the head clear off the first enemy who came into his path. Fallon, too, was lashing out with his sword with skill and determination.

Galdor cut down the first man who reached him with a growl, killing him instantly.

He could see they were outnumbered as increased numbers of men came out of the forest into the town, and he slithered into the darkness, leaving his men and the remaining Fomorians to their deaths.

He had no loyalty to any but himself, and he would not die today.

One by one, Tiernan and his men cut down the Fomorians and Galdor's men until the street was awash with the blood and death of their enemies.

The deafening screams faded, leaving an eerie silence ringing through all their ears.

As they gathered their minds, Cronan rushed to Tiernan's side in desperation. "Tiernan, they have taken the women and children out of the village a while ago. They marched east towards the castle," he continued, "my wife, my children are gone." Tiernan placed his hand on Cronan's shoulder before he spoke, looking around him at the men who had fallen in the battle remorsefully.

"Cronan, they will be okay; I feel Carman wishes to use them as a bargaining tool, and so long as she feels she can use them, they will be safe." Cronan nodded with a relieved sigh.

Tiernan patted him on his back and continued. "Rest regroup, and we will move out soon to catch up with the other clans and prepare for our greatest fight to come."

Chapter 12

Fiadh and Conn sat close by the opening of the Bru na Boinne as she explained in detail what they must do. "Conn, we have to travel this path alone, and Finian must travel back to prepare with Father and the other clans."

She continued, "As the future of this land, we are the only ones who can appeal to the Tuatha de Danann to leave their land and help fight Carman."

Conn's eyes had not left hers the entire time she spoke, and she shivered under his stare.

He was deep in thought. She could see that and knew he was forming a plan in his mind as he processed the rest of what she had told him.

He placed his hand on hers and breathed deeply before exhaling.

His muscular chest rose and fell as he said nothing and glanced towards the opening of the mound.

The storm was not affecting where they sat; they could see it off in the distance, yet it had not touched anything around them as though they were in a dream.

The sky was bright, and the grass was dry and lush. Everything felt so calm here. Conn was absorbing all that had happened, and all that Fiadh had told him.

He brushed his hand through his messy hair and looked back to Fiadh, now speaking as he held her hand. "We leave right now, Fiadh. Time is of importance as I fear Carman and her army may already be on the move."

He called Finian and the other men. "What is the plan, Conn?" Finian asked. Quickly, Conn explained what Fiadh had told him, and Finian and the other men nodded with understanding anxious expressions. They would not like leaving Conn and Fiadh without protection, but they knew Conn would not send them away if it were not necessary.

Fiadh pointed to the hollow in the tree. "Finian, you must use that for a swift journey back to my father." Finian looked at the opening in a tree, confused.

Fiadh spoke again, "Finian, there is no time to explain. Just trust me."

Finian nodded before replying. "With my life, I trust you, Fiadh." He bowed before giving her and Conn small embraces.

He called to the other men to follow him, and they walked towards the hollow in the tree.

Fiadh and Conn watched as they entered the opening and then could be seen no more.

Conn took Fiadh by her hand as they walked towards the opening in the Bru na Boinne mound.

The darkness engulfed them as they entered; their heads became dizzy, and they felt their minds become foggy. Conn wrapped his strong, firm hand tighter onto Fiadh's small, delicate hand, lacing their fingers onto each other.

Their eyes slowly adjusted. They moved at a quicker pace, looking at the walls of the passage. There were carvings all over them of great battles and hideous creatures fighting men of the clans.

There was a deep, sweet aroma surrounding them now, giving them a feeling of great tranquillity.

Out of nowhere, a great blast of wind hit them. Feeling like it had passed through their very souls.

Yet there was a great feeling of calm and safety now, and they pushed on for what seemed like hours. Their feet were sore, and the mud beneath them was becoming deeper and deeper as they sunk into it. Water began swirling around them, rapidly rising past their ankles to their knees.

The water rose higher and higher as Conn and Fiadh slipped under it, and they became submerged. They did not panic and allowed the water to carry them as they held onto each other. A great light appeared ahead of them, and the water disappeared as fast as it had risen. It grew brighter and more brilliant as they moved closer to what they could see was an opening at the end of the passage.

Conn stepped out first, holding Fiadh's hand tightly as he gazed out at the castle in front of him. His eyes widened in awe at this magnificent sight standing tall against the sky.

It was made of great grey stone with towers on four sides, stretching into the clouds above. It had a great wooden statue of a Stag standing tall on the wall, holding its head in a bow before its knee.

Fiadh knew immediately it was of Cernunnos, and she bowed low in respect. There was a bridge between them and the castle stretching out in front of them.

As they approached, they could hear the thunderous roar from the water below, yet all that could be seen as the vapour floating up towards them, hiding any bottom from view.

The bridge was covered with beautiful markings carved in it of horses, wolves, foxes, hares and giant ravens. Both of them recognized them as the gods' familiars. As they crossed the great bridge, a bellowing sound began to echo through the sky and fill it with the sounds of a haunting horn.

The enormous gates began to slide open, and a group of men marched out with gold masks, wearing gold leine covered in emeralds and garnets sewn into them. The jewels sparkled so brightly in the sun that they created a magical glow all around them as if it was protecting them.

Behind them, a woman stepped forward with a beauty that no other had ever seen. Her hair red as fire, her skin as white as snow.

By her side, two other women appeared, and they were as beautiful as the first.

A man slowly emerged draped in a cloak with the hood hiding his face. A long beard flowing out from beneath it. He was towering over the ladies, and they bowed low as his hems flowed past them.

Conn took a knee, and Fiadh bowed low as the man approached them and outstretched his hand, placing it on Conn's and Fiadh's heads.

He called for them to rise, and he stepped back, removing his hood staring down at them.

His eyes, the colour of blue ice, fixed on Fiadh, and he smiled a warm, strong smile through his full long blond beard. His voice boomed out from his chest, echoing across the valley.

"Welcome, Fiadh and Conn."

Tiernan marched with his men out into the forest and marshes to follow the path where they would meet up with the other clan leaders and prepare for the great battle.

He would take them through the Cong forest and onto the Cong caves, where they would have cover and shelter to make their plans.

The Aes Sidhe who resided there kept themselves quiet and unseen, but you could feel their very eyes burning onto the back of your neck.

Always waiting for a sign you could not be trusted and giving them leave to vent their magic on those who would give them the reason.

The trees were great oaks covered all over by furry moss travelling along the ground they walked on.

The rivers ran in all different directions in between the trees and made the ground marshy and dangerous for any who did not know the land as well as they did. This was the waters of Eriu that gave life to all their land.

Tiernan knew they were safe to move through here and did not expect any attack from Carman or her men, or they would meet their deaths without even a sword raised.

He could hear the low, shrilled whistle of the Aes Sidhe warning the others in the forest of intruders coming through. The wind in the trees howled loudly, brushing through every leaf being performed above them and all around as it danced into their ears. So long as they did not cut any trees or eat anything on this land, they were not a threat to the folk, and they would let them pass safely.

Tiernan knew better than anyone, having been descended from the Aes Sidhe himself on his father's side of the family.

Fairy folk, as they were once called, are rarely seen by the eyes of outsiders, only heard during the traditional Solstice's. They would play their hauntingly beautiful music that danced through the wind and trees across the land. Every soul could feel them and knew that it would bring healthy harvests and good fortune to all.

A true rarity, though, was a child born by the full moon on such a night as a Solstice. And he or she would be the gifted future true leaders of their land.

Tiernan's thoughts fell back to the night he and Aoife had been gifted with their beautiful daughter.

His heart even now welled up with the strongest of love and sadness with the memories of Aoife and Fiadh in his arms.

Fiadh was born on the night of the winter Solstice, and they knew she was going to be special.

Her magical connection with all animals and people was something to behold as a beauty within itself. All that she came in contact with were drawn to her caring nature, and they walked away from her with a feeling of hope. Her smile and her kindness were known throughout the land, and she was a protector of all in her heart. He smiled warmly.

She had become a well-loved and respected young woman. His heart winced a little, knowing how proud Aoife would be of their daughter, yet it hurt she was not there to see it herself.

Tiernan jumped when he heard a loud thud behind him, jumping with his sword drawn. In front of him stood a young woman with long, bright red hair and eyes as green as the moss under his feet.

She glowed in front of him as if a fire was engulfing her and all around, yet there was no heat. He raised his hand, trying to shade his eyes from the brilliance, and before he could ask who she was, he already knew.

Eriu, Goddess of the Tuatha de Danann, stood in front of him. He fell to a knee and placed his sword in front of him in honour of her.

Eriu's voice was almost like a whisper floating through his ears, yet she did not speak. He could hear her in his thoughts like a distant dream. "Tiernan, I have come to tell you Fiadh and Conn are safe far away with us."

Tiernan gasped in relief. She continued, "There will be a great fight in this time that we do not know the outcome. I give you one blessing as protection that I may as a descendant from your father of the Aes Sidhe."

Tiernan looked into her eyes and said, "My loyalties are to our land and people. I will fight to my last breath to keep our homes free from any who would destroy it." Eriu smiled a bright, warm smile and nodded happily, responding again

"I will give this weapon that can be used once. It must be used at the exact right time so that it may serve you in the way it is destined to."

She raised her hand, and with it appeared a spear shining bright silver. Its head was shaped like a leaf with three centred holes.

Placed in between each hole were three blue stones that shone bright even in the darkness. It stood on top of a long arm also made of silver, and Tiernan knew it was the Spear of Lugh.

Tiernan placed his sword at his waist and stepped forward, taking the spear in his hand.

He felt a sudden jolt rush through him, every essence of his soul and body connecting with it. In an instant, the visions of many who had fallen by the spear in the hands of Lugh became visions of almost reality in his mind. He stood back gasping and looked to see where Eriu was, to be seen no more.

Chapter 13

Carman marched on towards her destination and to what she was sure to be victory. She looked around, smiling. This time, she was not going to make the mistake of letting the strong survive.

Out of the forest ahead, two figures came running in their direction. She knew instantly it was her son.

She dismounted from the Cresocia and glided into the long blades of grass towards them.

Her mind was already a silent rage, "Why are her sons not still executing their observations of Tiernan."

Dother sniggered knowingly as he watched in silent satisfaction.

Dian and Dubh stopped moving when they saw their mother walking towards them. They could feel the unnatural silence fall around them as she moved across the open field. The wind picked up a mound of leaves, throwing them in a swirling, chaotic dance around her.

She stopped a distance from them and waved her hand in the air. Without even a word, she swiped down, and Dian fell to his knees, screaming out in a horrific wail.

It echoed through the sky above like thunder. The birds flew out of the trees in fright.

Across Dian's chest, blood oozed out through his clothing as he bent over, clutching it.

Dubh braced himself as Carman raised her hand again and swiped it down in an even more treacherous gesture. He screeched loudly and fell backward as blood poured out of one of his eyes, and he fell to the ground, clutching his face. Carman turned back to Dother and waved at him to have his brothers aided.

"No time to stop, load them up and keep moving," she shouted. No one took a second look and marched on.

As Conn and Fiadh were shown inside the large gates, they surveyed what they were seeing with amazement.

A city emerged in front of their eyes, many walkways with grey stone shelters stretching up them on either side. There were no people to be seen, but they could hear murmured voices from behind the closed doors as they passed.

Dagda, who they now knew they were following, did not speak any more and guided them slowly through the streets.

Lined with Cherry blossom trees next to each front door. It all seemed like a glorious dream to Fiadh and Conn as they tried to make sense of what they had found.

Eriu's eyes landed on Conn and Fiadh, smiling warmly as though she could read their thoughts and spoke for the first time.

"This is the land of the ascended souls, and you are gifted this entrance as you are both children of the Solstice."

She continued, "Only those who are of Tuatha de Danann or Aes Sidhe descent may enter. We are the link to the living and those who passed over."

Conn stared back in shock at her words, and Eriu placed her hand on his shoulder before speaking again.

"You and Fiadh are doubly blessed being children of the Solstice also."

Fiadh knew she was born on the Winter Solstice, but Conn had never mentioned he was also born on one.

Her eyes fell on him with a questioning look. Conn shrugged his shoulders before returning his gaze on the street ahead. Eriu interrupted the silence with her melodic voice.

"We know of your descent from Aes Sidhe also Fiadh. These things are vital so that you may use the instruments we give as gifts to you in your battle ahead."

They came upon a wide-open area with a statue of a beautiful woman standing gracefully in the centre, holding a jug in each hand, sparkling water poured from them onto the street, flowing off into the distance.

Dagda spoke all of a sudden, "This is Boann, the river Goddess." He smiled with a look of admiration when he said her name.

Conn and Fiadh knew all too well her story and how she died. He continued, "Her flowing waters feed the streams of our land and yours, nourish every living creature so that our land always flourishes."

He changed his direction, walking towards large hazelnut trees laid out in front of them like an arch. As they emerged from beneath their great branches to the other side, the enormity of the castle appeared in front of them.

Grey towers on four sides with pink flowers trailing along the walls around them. They continued inside to a great hall, where a large wooden table had been set with jugs and fruits of all sorts.

In the centre of the table, a great blue flame rose, flickering brightly. As they moved closer to the table, they noticed there was no heat from the flame, and yet they were warmed by its shadow.

Eriu gracefully glided across to one of the chairs, gesturing to them to sit down.

Fiadh and Conn moved to their seats, as did Dagda. Banba and Fodla appeared from another door before seating themselves across from them at the table.

Three men of great stature stood by each of the doors surrounding the room. They had silver masks hiding their faces beneath. You could only see their eyes shining a deep green from behind. Dagda gestured for Conn and Fiadh to eat with a warm smile. They had never seen such colours and so many fruits before.

Fiadh took a bite from one of the pieces of fruit; its sweet juices rolled along her tongue, and she almost sighed with pleasure.

Conn stared at her and blushed hard as he realised his mouth was open. She laughed hard, and he smiled warmly at her. The love they had for each other was obvious to any who saw them together.

Dagda interrupted the moment. "Now, the reason you are both here is to receive instruments to assist you in your coming battle." He nodded to one of the guards standing at the doors. He continued, "These items of great power are a legacy for our Land and will be in your charge until you are victorious."

Conn and Fiadh looked at each other, both knowing what items he was referring to.

Conn's hair stood up on his arms, and Fiadh shivered in anticipation.

The guard returned with two others carrying two items, draped in red sheathing and gold ties.

The other guards moved towards the table, removing the food that was left there.

Dagda rose from his seat as the guard handed him a long item, and he placed it on the table. Removing the ties, he spoke with considerable pride as he handed it to Conn. "This is the Claiomh Solais, the sword of light. Yielded by many great warriors and now by you in the greatest battle you will have ever fought."

Conn held out his hands as Dagda placed it across his palms. Conn gasped when he felt a jolt through his body. In front of his eyes, a flash of brilliant light and a sudden vision of a man yielding the same sword lashing out against a tall, dark shadow.

He felt the power of the darkness in front of him and the strength of the man holding the sword.

All around him, he could hear the clashing of swords and roars of a great battle. Then, silence as the man carrying the sword paused, looking over in Conn's direction.

He was wearing a silver helmet covering his whole face so that you could only see his eyes peering out at him.

His green cloak floated out against a gust of wind falling over his shoulder and settling around his chest. He looked like a giant in the night as he strides swiftly towards Conn.

Conn felt unsure if he was now dreaming or had he collapsed with the jolt he felt from the sword.

A loud booming voice brought him back to his surroundings as a thick fog rolled in around them, rising up as if from moss beneath their feet.

"Conn, I am Nuada."

Conn could hardly believe his ears, and he stared in astonishment. Nuada continued, "I bestow on you the great gift of Claiomh Solais. While this is a tool of war and has won many a victory against great evil, it is also," Nuada sighed loudly. "It is a legacy and a great honour to be given to you."

Conn looked back into his hands, and although Nuada was still holding the sword, Conn was too.

Nuada continued, "You have a strong enemy to fight, and she is not one of the human lands any more.

You are the only one who can protect Fiadh and our people from Carman's wish to destroy all that is good about our land. You must be prepared for the fight to restore peace across the land."

Conn spoke quietly, unsure he was not in a delusion of some kind. "I will fight to my last breath for my people and our home."

Nuada placed his hand on Conn's head as Conn felt a jolt and was back in the great hall with Fiadh. Her face was one of worry and shock as he reappeared in front of her.

"Where did you go?" She exclaimed as she threw her arms around him. He then knew he had been thrown out of their time, and it was no dream or hallucination.

Dagda spoke again as he placed the second item in front of Fiadh, "This is Uaithne, My most powerful weapon.

No one can withstand its music, and you will know when the time has come to use it." Fiadh removed the velvet cover, and standing on the table in front of her was a Harp.

Her eyes widened in awe at its beauty. It was made from a dark brown wood and small enough for her to carry over her shoulder.

It had carved lines falling along the arm with gold-painted stripes in circular shapes along the sides. The strings were made from the finest threads of gold that glittered in the light shining in from the window above.

At the front, there was a figure of a beautiful woman carved into it, whose yellow hair stretched down the front beyond her legs.

Fiadh knew this was Leanan Sidhe of the fairy folks. The stories of her were long told around the fires at night. She loved human men, and although she did not wish them harm, her love aged them faster, and they would die within ten years. She cried for all she loved until she found a new love.

Dagda spoke again, "Yes, the voice of Leanan Sidhe is the melody inside Uaithne and is mesmerising to all who hear it. She is also known to be the banshee and cries hardest of all when she knows death is to befall on anyone. She loves most true and grieves just as strongly."

Eriu spoke sweetly, placing her hand on Fiadh's arm, "Fiadh, come with me, and you may rest and bathe. It has been a long, tiresome few days for you."

Conn stood up to protest against being separated. Eriu spoke with a soft voice, "Conn, you will be in the room next to Fiadh, so you will not be far from her. I assure you she is safer here than anywhere."

Eriu led the pair out a door and into a long hallway with torches lined along the wall.

Many doors stretched down the corridor, with music flowing from behind each one as they passed them.

She glided gracefully in front of them until they stopped in front of a great wooden door with carvings of great oaks in it.

Eriu gestured to Fiadh to step in as she pushed the door open.

Fiadh was astonished as she stepped into a gigantic room with a bed bigger than any she had ever seen.

The bed had four wooden posts reaching up high above their heads and flowing gold material draping down on each side.

There was a great window high up on the wall, illuminating the room in all corners. A large table sat across the other side of the room with a glowing item standing in the middle of it, held up by two branches shaped into hands.

She moved across to look at this strange object and realised she could see her own reflection in it. It was like looking in the rivers, yet this did not ripple or move.

Fiadh reached out, touching it softly. She gasped a little in surprise and touched her own face, watching her reflection do the same.

Conn watched on in surprise, too. He leaned in, looking first at himself, slowly moving his eyes to linger on Fiadh. Her eyes met his in the reflection, and they smiled lovingly at each other.

Eriu spoke up as she moved to a door at the side of the room,

"Conn, this is your room over here, so you are at all times close to Fiadh." she continued. "I will leave you both to settle and rest a while. You have perilous endeavours ahead." With that, she smiled and exited, leaving Fiadh and Conn alone.

Fiadh reached her hand out, intertwining her fingers in Conn's. The connection between them had always been intense. He stared into her eyes with so much devotion, and she knew he would always be there for her.

His hand glided along her hair, gently sliding it across her cheek, speaking as he stroked her cheek. "My Fiadh, I was so scared I had lost you forever!"

She cupped her hand around his that lay on her cheek and sank into it as if he was holding her whole body in just his hand.

He always had the power in his eyes, how he looked at her to make her feel like the most special and beautiful woman in the world. Her heart soared every time he spoke her name.

He slowly leaned in and kissed her so softly her skin tingled, and she shivered right down to her soul.

Conn stepped back, looking into her eyes, mesmerising every fleck of blue that danced in them. He brushed a stray hair away from her cheek and spoke. "Fiadh, please take a rest now, and I will be in the next room. You can call me if you need me."

Fiadh grasped Conn's hand and slowly moved towards the great bed beside them. "Please do not leave me, Conn. I need to know you are by me while I sleep." Conn followed her as she lay down on the bed, and he slid in beside her. She faced him and snuggled her head into his chest. He enclosed her body into him like a butterfly in its cocoon. They slowly drifted into a deep sleep.

Chapter 14

The night grew still, and everyone on the land was bracing themselves for what lay ahead. The women, young and old, hid in any secret location they could find.

They knew their husbands and sons would be fighting a great battle soon, and they looked to Cernunnos for protection on their behalf.

Aodh and Cillian halted their people in the tunnels for a rest as they knew the air was thick in there. They all collapsed against the walls in relief, rubbing their weary feet as Cronan and other men moved around with water.

It was a long journey still to the next opening for them. They could not be sure if Carman and her men would be moving across the top of them. They feared she may sense them somehow, and they would be discovered.

Cronan moved to his father's side and looked at him with questioning eyes before speaking. "Should we not have stayed and fought alongside Tiernan?" he asked. His father paused, staring intensely at his son and nodded. "We do not question Tiernan's orders of what we must do. The people are in danger, and we must keep them safe for the future of the land in case anything goes wrong."

Cronan was hungry to prove himself in a battle, and he felt robbed of his chance. He scoffed under his breath at his father's words and slid back against the wall, looking at the roots in the mud above him. He imagined the victory he could have been a part of and the stories told in years to come, how his name would not be told in future lore.

Aodh knew how Cronan's urge to prove himself had made him impulsive and lacking foresight in any battle. He was young and eager, but Aodh was not ready to let his son fight any great evil unless he showed himself for maturity that was needed. Tiernan had agreed to keep Cronan with Aodh for these exact reasons.

He may have to fight sooner than they hoped, but for now, he would keep him in his watchful eyes and guide him to make stronger, wiser decisions.

Finian and his men had stepped through the great oak Fiadh had directed them to.

It seemed like a whisper when they came out the other side by the perimeter of Cong forest.

The storm had grown wilder in their time at Bru na Boinne, and seemed like they had stepped into another land.

The darkness had overtaken their land again, and the rain fell loud and hard on everything around them.

Finian did not question how or why they had come out so far from their homes. He looked to his men and raised his hand to follow him as he led them into the forest of the Aes Sidhe.

His men looked a little disconcerted at the thought of entering the forest without being given an invitation.

Finian stood tall, addressing them confidently,

"Cernunnos put us on this path for a reason. We do not question that and follow what is shown to us." With that above them, they heard a loud cawing, and Morrigu sailed over the tree lines in the direction of Aes Sidhe's home.

They could not see her, but they had no doubt in their minds she had re-joined them to show the way. They gathered their courage again and stepped out into the oncoming wind and rain, into the land no one dared to enter.

Morrigu stretched out her wings and scanned the land surrounding the woods. Her eyes could see far from where she was through the eyes of other earthly creatures.

She could see the Carman's underlings crossing through many fields, searching to create death and destruction.

She wanted to lash out and destroy all in her path, but she could not without causing death to all on the land.

She remained untouched by the forceful storm blowing around her and watched protectively over Finian and his men until they would come to safety with Tiernan.

Finian gave the orders as had Tiernan, "Do not touch, harm or break anything in this land, or you will no longer be welcome by the Aes Sidhe." All nodded in agreement.

They battled through the wind and rain, blasting their every step until all went calm and quiet out of nowhere.

They had come between great boulders surrounded by trees. Although the rain continued to lash, the wind no longer caused any hindrance to their progress. In the distance, they could see figures moving towards them, and they slowed their pace, edging now cautiously forward.

A booming voice called out beyond the trees, "Finian."

He knew instantly it was his father, Fallon, and he had a sudden feeling of relief to know his father was alive.

A group of men rushed forward, grabbing their sons and patting them on the back, all happy to see each other. Finian's father stepped forward and embraced his son hard, stepping back and looking at him proudly. "Son, it is good to see you and your men safe."

Tiernan stepped out from behind Fallon, his eyes asking questions without speaking a word. Finian stepped forward, speaking clearly, "Fiadh is well, and she travelled with Conn to visit the Tuatha de Danann."

Tiernan nodded and smiled before turning to the rest of the men and calling out his orders.

"We move to the Cong caves to meet with our kin and prepare for battle."

They moved out in groups, talking low amongst each other, aware they were still not out of the woods yet. Tiernan's mind was at last resting, knowing Fiadh was safe with Conn, even though Eriu told him already.

He was glad to hear it from one of his kin; it brought him peace. Now they could really concentrate on the battle ahead, and Fiadh was, for now, out of harm's way.

Finian spoke to Tiernan as they made their way through the forest, "Fiadh turned up at Bru na Boinne with two great creatures in the skin of wolves." Tiernan flicked his eyes onto Finian, not at all surprised by this revelation.

He was familiar with Con-ri and Cuan from the stories his father had told him of generations past.

He had never physically seen them until he heard of the birth of Conn.

Conn was born on the day of the Alban Hefin (The Light of Shore). He had long known Conn was also a child of the Solstice, and this always came with great burdens in adult life.

His second time seeing them was the night Fiadh was born. The snow had fallen hard on that Grianstad night. It had covered every tree and mountain within view and surrounding. It brightened up the winter night with a great white hue and pinkest sky he had ever seen.

Not even the moon or the stars shone brighter. The fire burned bright in the centre of the room as Aoife called out in pain, giving birth to their beautiful baby girl Fiadh. Tiernan looked out upon the forest when he felt a presence watching their home, and there they were. Two great wolves standing on top of the hill in the middle of the forest.

Tiernan knew that day Fiadh would always be guarded by the Gods, and he also knew there would be great trials ahead for her.

He also realised that night, two children born on Solstice celebration days would be destined to be together in the future. That is when Conn's father and Tiernan made a pact to bring them together when they were old enough to be wed.

Tiernan had never divulged this information to either of them. After what happened with Conn's parents, he didn't feel there was a need to any more. They had been drawn to each other without anyone ever having to make it happen.

Tiernan had been preparing them both for this day all their lives, and his heart ached, knowing that this was written before they even were born.

No one had known when it would come to pass, as the story had been passed down generation to generation. It was spoken of over the years that two children born on the Solstice would be the ones to fight the threat that would befall their land and people.

Now it had come, Tiernan knew it was this story he had heard so many times but never imagined it would be his little girl who would have to take on this kind of battle.

The whistling continued swirling around their ears as they marched through the forest on their way to the Cong caves. High pitched with a harmonious touch to it, lulling the men into a state of ease.

Tiernan could see the end of the tree lines and the wind picking up. It moaned loud and angrily as though it knew their land was being threatened. They looked back into the woods as they stepped out in front of the caves.

There was great light floating amongst the trees and many figures standing tall looking at them. Tiernan nodded in thanks to them for the safe passage through their land, as did all the men who accompanied him, and with that, the shadows of the Aes Sidhe vanished into a swirling mist floating up into the trees until gone.

Tiernan looked back towards the caves and raised his arm to move forward to the opening.

Fiadh awoke to a glorious sun shining through the great window above her head.

She raised her arms up, stretching and groaned, feeling her aching bones shift and crack. Even though she had slept quite well, she still felt the effects of her treacherous journey.

Suddenly, her mind leapt, and she twisted in a panic, searching for Conn, to meet his eyes staring right at hers and smiling warmly.

She whispered his name softly, and he kissed her lips delicately.

Her whole body shivered under his gaze, and she loved him so completely it was like freedom for her.

Conn slid his fingers through her hair, trailing down across her neck, and he tingled to be so close to her. Her eyes swept along his muscular frame, and she trickled her fingers across his chest.

He bit his lip and moved his hands to her face before lifting himself off the bed and grabbing his leine, placing it over his head.

Her eyes looked confused and disappointed. He wanted her so much, but he would not take this pleasure until they were joined in union.

A knock came on the door with a sweet voice calling out from behind it, "Fiadh, Conn, it's time for you to reunite with Tiernan. Please come."

Fiadh looked excited and worried all at once, and Conn placed his hand in hers, helping her off the bed. "Get dressed, Fiadh. It's time to take our home and lives' back."

She moved quickly across the room. Conn's eyes lingered on her graceful body with fire in his soul.

She found a Leine draped across the chair of a brilliant white and gold in colour, made of the finest silk she had ever seen.

It slipped down her naked body like the rain dancing off the leaves on a spring day, light and soft.

Her beauty for him matched no other, and he would die protecting her if he must, he thought. Fiadh slid her fingers across her clothing and placed a white robe around her shoulders.

She looked at the item on the table by her side, silver in colour and realised it was her comb from her room.

The carved markings of their family line plain as day. Confused but not at all surprised, she brushed her brown hair until it was once again sleek and shining.

She lifted two parts of her hair and fixed her comb on the back of her head, holding it back. She turned to Conn and said, "I want us to be in union today before we leave so that we may not be ever parted if this day ends in our deaths."

Conn's heart sped up in his chest with happiness and fear at her words. He stepped towards her and placed his hand in hers, "With every breath in my body, from the depth of my soul as the Gods see me now, would you honour me by being my one true love always." Fiadh grasped his face in her hands and kissed him amorously, smiling through her kisses as tears of joy fell down her cheeks.

Conn licked his lips as one of her tears fell on them, and he embraced her tightly to his body.

From behind, a voice called out, "Come with me if we are to join you in union before you leave." Eriu had entered the room and was smiling with delight at what she had heard.

"It has been a very long time since we have seen a union of such in our land."

She linked Conn's arm and whisked him out the door as she looked over her shoulder, calling out.

"We will be with you soon to prepare you." With that, the door closed behind her and Conn.

Fiadh, now alone with her thoughts, was so happy at the thoughts of being tied to Conn always and terrified of what lay before them in the coming days.

She barely had a moment before four women burst into the room with ribbons, silks and flowers.

They ushered her into a room of hers that had a deep hole in the ground made of white stone.

Before she could say a word, water started to pour from a wooden pipe hanging over it.

The steam flowed through the room and filled it quickly.

The ladies, who all wore white hooded wraps, called to Fiadh to undress and enter the water. She did so hesitantly and smiled when her first foot sank into its warmth. She slowly sunk into the water and felt all her aches soothing to the heat, laying back with a sigh of relief.

One of the women started to wash Fiadh's hair, rubbing it softly. The other women spoke softly with kindness. "Fiadh, you are going to make the most beautiful bride." Fiadh smiled, feeling the glow of red on her face, thinking of when she would be Conn's wife.

She felt sadness that her father and friends would not be there for it. She knew he would agree that now was the time.

Fiadh climbed out of the water and was wrapped in a soft cloth as they dried her and combed her hair. Already, her stomach was doing flips with excitement, and she knew once they were bonded for life, they would be stronger than ever.

Eriu returned, gliding across the floor as if she didn't even touch the ground carrying a gown of such beauty, Fiadh gasped.

Eriu placed it in Fiadh's arms and asked her to put it on.

She slid her hands along its delicate fabric in awe at how soft it was to the touch. It was as white as the Wild Morning Glory that grew across the land.

It had blue trim reaching around the waist, meeting in the middle, flowing down the centre and along the hem, made up with the bluest jewels she had ever seen.

She slid the dress over her head, and it fell delicately around her body. It was a low cut along her chest, clinging to her neatly, showing her every curve. The sleeves covered her whole arm as a blue cloth fell from the wrist to the elbow, flowing out underneath like the wings of a bird. Fiadh raised her arms and twirled gently, smiling delightfully.

Eriu smiled while watching and whispered, "Let us do your hair, dear Fiadh."

She took her hand and led her to a stone bench in front of the object that reflected her image. Eriu smiled and nodded at Fiadh, saying, "This is a looking glass, Fiadh."

Fiadh responded. "I have seen myself often in the reflection of many waters, but I've never seen myself as clearly as if I am looking at another me. Almost like I could reach out and touch her, and I would feel her."

Fiadh heard the giggles from behind her. Eriu's face twisted from great beauty to dark and, for the first time, looked stern.

Her eyes had a shadow evolve around them, and her voice became cold and dangerous, "Be quiet. Do you realise who you dare insult by giggling like stupid children?"

They froze on the spot and looked to their toes in embarrassment.

Eriu had been nothing but soft and gentle until now, and Fiadh was reminded she was in the presence of the Gods and not just a kindly woman.

Eriu looked back at Fiadh and smiled again, looking light and soft. She lifted two pieces of Fiadh's long brown hair and began to plait it back off her face, leaving the majority to fall down her back loose. One of the girls brought forward a white head piece shaped like a half-moon with the same blue jewels draped around it and placed it on her head.

The girls all stared at her with smiles of adoration at this beautiful sight in front of them.

"Now you are ready to join with Conn," Eriu smiled and reached for Fiadh's arm, leading her towards the door.

Chapter 15

Galdor caught up with Carman and Dother, ready to give his update on how they had lost all those Fomorians and some of his men to Tiernan's onslaught. He was now scared, as she may think he failed since he had survived.

He took his knife and slashed at his arm and leg to show he had battled hard. He then took his knife and, drew it across his cheek, and cut. All cuts he made were only slight.

Enough to show a lot of blood but not enough to cause him any real danger.

He shifted uneasily with the pain he had inflicted on himself. It was necessary to hide his abandonment of his men back in the town.

Less injury than what Carman would cause him if she ever suspected him of his treachery. He bided his time until she no longer suited his needs.

He fell out of the trees behind Carman and her followers, calling out loudly.

The forces all halted. None turned around to see who was behind them. From down the line, Galdor could see the tall figure of Dother striding towards him.

He was not expecting any sympathy from him or Carman, and he knew he would probably be punished for his failure.

Yet he hoped that with these wounds so obvious, he would not be instantly killed and again be able to continue with his plan. Dother now stood over him, threateningly, showing anger etched across his long, hard face.

Galdor spoke low with conviction. "Dother, we were attacked by Tiernan. He came out of the forest like spirits of the dead."

They cut all down. He caught his breath to make it sound more believable; "I only made it out by the strength of my will to bring you the news and serve you and high goddess Carman." Dother sneered down at him before raising his arm, lashing it down on Galdor with a great might. Galdor screeched out in pain and kneeled at Dother's feet.

He spoke loudly in a hostile tone. "You have failed me once, Galdor; you fail again, and you will not be given another chance." Galdor looked up and nodded in understanding. He did not speak, but in his mind, he was sniggering at this fool who he had no loyalty to.

He was safe again for now and would use Carman's army to reap his riches and victory when the time came.

Dother stepped away, moving off towards his mother. He knew Galdor was merely using them to get riches and had no loyalty to him or his mother. Galdor was merely a useful tool because of his men, and when the time came, Dother would enjoy slaying them all.

He moved up to the front with his mother and looked up at her. Dother called to her, "My queen, Tiernan has taken back his town and men. All the Formorians and men I left behind are dead or taken except Galdor." Her eyes twisted in a knowing gesture; she already knew he had abandoned his post, and she growled low under her breath.

They marched on at a faster pace, seeing the peaks of the castle reaching out amongst the trees ahead. Her destination was Tiernan's home, and to use what people her men had gathered in the few days from other towns as bait.

She would conquer Tiernan and take back this land once more, but this time, she would not fail.

The women and children were shackled and travelled in the middle of the Formorians out of reach of any rescue.

She knew other clans would be travelling to assist Tiernan in his fight, and she would not underestimate them.

Her mind fell back to the days she was imprisoned in this very castle in the pits.

How frail she had become from the treatment they had bestowed on her. She slept in the dirt on hard, cold ground. The smell hurt her nose when she breathed. She did not know how many years she was held there.

There was no light to tell day from night or winter from summer, as it was always cold and dark. The rats surrounded her, scratching and biting her weak, broken skin.

They fought her for the morsel of food thrown at her through a hole in the door. No one spoke to her for many moons until she was surrounded by darkness.

She was in pain alive, and then she was nowhere, suffering in the murk of nothingness. Then, all of a sudden, she had an awakening in another land by the hand of Dother, her son.

He had stolen her body back in the darkness from where they had dumped her.

No fire for her soul so that she may transcend to the afterlife.

He had brought her back with the power of dark enchantments, and she now, too, had transcended to a higher life beyond humans.

As she stared off in the direction of the Castle, she grasped her dagger tight in her hand.

She was thinking of the moment she would plunge it into the heart of the descendants that killed her.

Not long now, she thought to herself and let out a nasty cackle that echoed through the trees and sent all around into an icy silence.

The Fomorians shuffled quickly between each other, faces stern and misshapen, focused only on death and chaos. Like their minds, they marched in a disorderly manner without any formation.

They fought in the same way, but this time, they had a powerful leader who did not think the same and fought in patterns.

They felt this time, they would be victorious and regain this land, standing on the necks of the people here.

Their smell insulted Galdor's nose as he marched behind them, and he thought what brutal-looking creatures he was surrounded by. His mind was always on victory, riches, and tasting the flesh of the young and the powerful.

He sucked in some air and licked his lips, thinking of Tiernan's power he would consume.

He chuckled quietly to himself, watching this swarm of Fomorian's and the horde of his own greedy, vicious men feeling empowered.

Nothing was sacred to them. Just what they could control and take is all that mattered to them.

I will not stay in this miserable land when I have turned it into a sea of fire and misery that which they've never seen, he thought.

Carman has other ideas for this land to rule and to take them as her servants. He would take as many lives as he could.

Since he was a young man, he revelled in death and enjoyed the feast afterward. His power came from their flesh, and he believed the more powerful the body, the stronger he became. Formorians were weak-minded creatures, feasting on anything that came to their mouths.

Tiernan and his men stepped out in front of the caves, staring down deep into the mouth of the opening. He struck a flint again and again up to the torch Fallon held up for him. The flame ignited, and one by one, a man stepped forward, lighting their torches. Tiernan stepped forward, lighting up the way, showing long stone-jagged steps leading far inside.

The darkness gave way to their shadows floating like dancing fairies on the walls.

They edged their way slowly down further and further until they could hear voices mumbling below.

Tiernan led them out into a large cavity, where many men sat around a great fire whispering quietly. Surrounding them were hundreds of men sleeping or sitting in groups huddled in discussions.

They looked up to see Tiernan and his men arrive and cheered in unison. "No watch on the mouth of the cave, Kyra. That is very risky of you, my friend." Tiernan called out towards the men sitting around the fire.

A very large man stood up, his hair down to his waist, grey and brown in colour, with a beard almost as long as his hair on his head. His steely glare landed on Tiernan as he bounded forward stealthy, stopping inches from Tiernan's face.

He growled under his breath, "You would call me risky? Tiernan. Dare you insult me, a king in his own right." His mountainous chest rising and falling as he stared at Tiernan. He continued, "Your eyes are fooling you, my dear friend, as did all of your men's eyes. It is ye who are risky." And he laughed.

Out of one corner, Tiernan spotted movement as the whites of eyes appeared coming out of the stone wall, one at first, then three more, one by one.

Hidden from their eyes, Kyra again had shown his skill. "I am impressed! Kyra, not even one of my best men saw them," Tiernan replied.

"They have been with you from the moment you stepped out of the woods and have been following you the whole time," Kyra replied.

The four men stepped forward into the light of the torches, their bodies covered in grey mud.

Tiernan laughed a big, gruffly chuckle and turned to Kyra. The two men laughed out loud together.

"Back to what has brought us to this urgent meeting," Tiernan spoke loudly as he moved across the Cave to the large rocks placed around the fire.

Lugh and Ruairi stood to greet him. The four men sat back down and stared over the flames at each other. Everyone stood behind them, all their shadows dancing off the rock face like an eerie tale. No one moved or spoke while their chiefs were making their plans. They listened intently to all.

Their faces were all so serious as they nodded in agreement with the plans that were being set out.

Ruairi spoke up over the rest of the men, "When is Fiachra coming? We all want to know?"

Tiernan stood up and spoke loudly so all could hear him, "We have sent for him, but he may not arrive on time.

We have to make our plans fit for us and not count on Fiachra until he is here." This time, Lugh spoke in a mumbled tone.

"Majority of us are not fighting men and have children and wives to worry about. If we die in a battle, what is to protect them from the witch and her beasts?"

Tiernan sighed before raising his voice. "If you do not fight, there will be no chance of victory, and they will still be in danger from these invaders." He continued, "We have the Tuatha de Danann on our side and this."

From behind, Tiernan could hear the low chatter and feeling of uncertainty from some of the men. He understood as they were not reared as fighters. He knew they were strong and descended from fighters.

He had not planned to pull the spear of Lugh out for show, but it was called for now to inspire bravery.

As he raised his hand in the air, the spear sprouted out in its full glory, lighting up the whole cavern. The men stared in surprise and wonder at this revelation and cheered in unison.

They began to chatter amongst themselves, feeling more confident in the future conflict they must face. The four men looked at each other, all knowing the spear was not going to win it for them.

They were happy to have the men's belief restored in their victory. Tiernan placed the spear by his side, still emitting a warm light around it. The other Chieftains stared at it, still unsure what they were seeing was real.

They settled back into their plan of attack, laying out their strategies and where to put them into play.

They ate and spoke amongst themselves late into the night until the fire dimmed, and silence fell across the cavern as the men, one by one, fell asleep.

The sparks floated from the fire as the embers began to fade, sailing to the roof and flickering out. Fallon shifted, poking the fire with a stick stirring up a raging flame shooting upwards. It was one they would need to form the strength for what lay ahead.

Two days and two nights of travelling in the hidden passageways, Aodh, Cillian and Cronan, along with all the women and children, had finally reached the end of the tunnels. It had been a long, hard, cold journey, but it was one of necessity. It was only a few hours walk to Ben Gorm and the safety hidden in the fortified mountains.

Cronan was still tormenting his father about his usefulness in an oncoming battle, and how he wanted to go back now they were safe out of the witches' clutches. Aodh grew weary and snapped at Cronan in a heated moment. "Stop your childish whining and man up to your responsibilities, Cronan," he said. Cronan stopped talking and grumbled low under his breath as he walked away to the back of the group.

His father was nothing more than an old man, he thought to himself, constantly trying to control him.

Cronan didn't like this at all, and his plan was formed. When they reached Ben Gorm, he was going to slip away and return to the fight. Cillian watched Cronan's face, knowing something was working in the young man's mind, and he would need to keep a watchful eye on him.

He nodded his head to a very burly man sitting in the corner, also watching Cronan with a questionable eye.

He caught Cillian's nod, acknowledging without even words he understood. Taibhse was a very quiet man; his fiery red hair and beard always unkempt, and he smelled like he had rolled in the bogs every day to bathe.

However, he was strong and fought with the heart of twenty men.

Cillian knew he could count on him to keep an eye on Cronan's wayward temperament if he lost sight of him.

Aodh interrupted Cillian's thoughts, "Cillian time to go up and make our way to Ben Gorm." Cillian nodded and moved towards a dark wall in front of him. With the aid of three other men, they began pushing.

The mud over their heads started to give way, falling on them as the boulder began to shift.

There was low, worried gasps from behind them as more and more mud began to fall all around them and the group. Aodh hushed them in an agitated tone, and they became silent.

There was a loud crunch from the sides of the boulder, and it finally slid away, letting a blast of wind whistle through the passage, making an ear-piercing groan. One of the women screamed, "We will all die. It's the banshee."

Aodh turned to her with his steely eyes, unimpressed with her outburst, and she looked to the ground ashamed immediately. All the women and children now looked terrified at the possibility of death awaiting them beyond the passages.

Aodh stepped up to the front of the opening, speaking loudly so everyone could hear him.

"Now, what would be this superstition? Causing fear for no reason. It is nothing but the wind and years of that boulder lodged in the mud." He continued, "I will hear nothing more about any of this talk." And he growled low in the woman's direction.

She slunk back into the group, hiding out of his gaze, and he turned, waving his arm for them to move out.

As they stepped out of the passages, they were met with the snow blowing hard, swirling wildly around them. The women wrapped themselves and the children tighter into their surcoats. It was night, and yet everything was bright as if daytime, almost blinding to their eyes after being underground for so long. Aodh looked ahead of him, but he could not see the peaks of Ben Gorm because of the blizzard.

The snow covered every blade of grass and tree in sight. He stroked his beard, thinking deeply. The children giggled with excitement at the icy sight they beheld and wanted to run and play.

They had no concept of real danger and thought they were untouchable. He wished he could go back to those days and let them, he thought to himself.

The snow lashed harder and harder, bashing into their faces and making them red and sore. Cronan spoke loudly, "Get back into the passage until the snow eases."

He looked to his father, almost afraid to see his reaction. To his relief, his father nodded in agreement, and everyone moved back inside for cover.

Aodh stood in the bitter cold, considering his options as Cronan stood by his side.

Cronan spoke quietly, "We could go ahead and make a track in the snow to clear the way for you and the others to make it safer?"

Aodh nodded, adding. "Bring Cillian and Taibhse with you, my son." Cronan smiled, for the first time in many months, with this new responsibility his father had given him, and he felt like it was the start to him being trusted to be the man he wanted to be.

Cillian, Cronan and Taibhse stepped back out into the snow storm, pulling a giant log behind them to dig a track into the snow.

The only problem was if any of Carman's men ventured this way, they may give away their hiding place.

Their hope was the snow would cover their tracks enough and all evidence of them passing through this way except for those who knew it would be there.

They had only one other choice: to stay in the passages until the snow stopped, but they had no food or water. The decision had been made, and they would follow when it wasn't so perilous for the young and old.

Aodh watched his son disappear slowly into the white night, wishing for the safety of his son and his companions.

His heart was proud of Cronan stepping up and making suggestions to help keep his people safe. He was finally showing himself as the man Aodh had always known was underneath the childish acts, he thought to himself.

Chapter 16

Conn stepped in front of the looking glass after he had bathed, preparing for his union with Fiadh. Many bruises from battle etched across his muscular structure had turned dark black over the days since.

He took his blade and cut into his scraggly, dirty blond hair, it as best he could. His piercing blue eyes shone wildly, looking back at him, thinking of the moment when it would be official.

A woman entered the room carrying a white tunic with blue trim and a fur-lined surcoat of grey and white. She placed a black belt on top of them and spoke without flinching at his nakedness. "It is almost time, please get dressed, and I will bring you to the hall." Conn could feel his heartbeat leap and thud hard and fast in his chest at the mere thought of being with Fiadh always.

Dressing quickly, he glanced at his image staring back at him and could not believe it was him. Eriu popped her head in the door and called out to Conn. "Come, Fiadh is ready for you!"

He followed her out the door and down a long hallway covered in white flowers.

The doors of the great hall opened slowly. Inside, there was a crowd of strangers dressed in glorious colours, smiling and staring at him.

He held his chest out and his head up as he walked inside, and from the side, Fiadh appeared. Her eyes sparkled with love as they locked with his, smiling softly as she gracefully moved towards him, placing her hand in his.

His eyes lingered on the vision of beauty that stood by his side, and he could not believe how lucky he was to earn her love.

He whispered in her ear, "Fiadh, the gods created you, and you are a goddess to me." Fiadh squeezed his hand and kissed his cheek, whispering in his ear, "I am only a goddess because you make me feel like one."

He turned his eyes to the top of the hall where Dadga stood wearing a gold robe. On his face was a gold mask covering just his eyes. They walked towards him, hearing the whispered words of admiration, "What a beautiful couple they are."

Behind Dadga was the great Blue Flame of life. It danced and flickered almost like it was playing a melody.

A tall woman stepped out beside Dagda and sang an old song that Fiadh had heard her mother sing when she was small, and her heart lifted, knowing this was a sign she was with her.

There was a circle of stones surrounding Dagda, with a break in the circle for Conn and Fiadh to enter.

As they stepped inside, two men moved in behind them and closed it off with branches entwined in each other. Dagda gestured to them to step closer as he reached and took both their hands, speaking so all could hear him.

"On this day, we bring our two children of the Solstice together in union under the Blue flame. It was written they would be born for each other, and their love would protect and bring balance to our land when the time was right. Their union is one of destiny seeded in the very dirt of our cherished home."

He continued, "Now I speak to you, Fiadh, Conn, please speak your words, that you may be bonded before the Blue Flame and protected."

Conn kneeled before Fiadh, taking his sword and placing it before her feet, gazing at her with devotion,

"I vow my body and soul to you, Fiadh of the wild. Daughter of Tiernan and Aoife, most beautiful, kind and gentlest of hearts.

I give you my life to do with it what you wish and will protect you with it." Fiadh smiled warmly, her love illuminating her as she bent her knees to reach Conn's level. "I vow my love and loyalty always to you, Conn, most brave, strongest of hearts."

She continued, "I will stand by your side and listen to your words with grace without question. We will guide each other in our journey ahead," they said in unison.

Dagda spoke again, "Conn, Fiadh, may you be united forever and protected by the Blue Flame of life."

Around the hall, the people began to cheer as Conn leaned over and kissed Fiadh softly, and she tingled from her head to toe with happiness.

Carman bellowed out her orders with malice, "Take the castle, and all inside tonight will not be given any leniency." The Fomorians rushed forward, their penetrating shrieks echoing out across the land.

The men inside the castle covered their ears, unable to move, falling to their knees.

Galdor held his place with his men, watching in excitement as the onslaught began.

There were men on the walls; they would take them fast, he was sure, without much fight.

The closer the Fomorians got to the castle, Carman's face twitched as she noticed there didn't seem to be much movement.

At the back of the castle, the men were already retreating through the entrance, hidden from the eye.

Cathal, whom Tiernan left in charge, was watching from the walls with twenty other volunteers.

They had placed figures who looked like bodies on the wall holding spears to convince the witch and her men there were people still there. It would keep her attention off the men leaving to re-join Tiernan.

Cathal raised his hand, and the other men fired their arrows high into the air, racing like the wind hitting the first of the Fomorians. Two fell, and another and another as more arrows shot out from the top of the castle walls.

Carman grinned wickedly, leaning to her right, whispering to Dother, "Merely a distraction. There must be men making their escape out somewhere else." Dother understood immediately what she wanted and turned to the men closest to him. "Spread out around the castle and look for the escaping savages and cut them down," he ordered.

A group of men shifted in different directions, moving out to engulf the castle in a ring shape.

Cathal could see their error. He knew the men had no hope if they were caught. He needed to think fast and smart. It was time to come face to face with their foe.

He looked to his other men and shouted, "Abandon the wall, men. We need to buy time for the others to get away back to Tiernan."

They knew this was death for them, and they were ready to give their lives to protect the others.

Each man ran swiftly down from the walls and out into the courtyard, yielding their swords.

The ground was thick with mud and straw, making their progress slow and unbalanced.

Cathal made it to the gate first and, with the ten other men, opened the gate, racing out swords raised and ready to die if it was meant to be. The other ten men ran to the back of the castle to where the secret opening was located.

They could see their friends running into the forest behind, disappearing into the darkness to safety.

The men Carman had sent to intercept them came roaring from either side with their swords raised. They cut down three of Tiernan's men straight away as the others fought hard to stay alive and keep them distracted from their escaping friends.

A barrage of Formorians fell upon Cathal as he lifted his sword, swinging hard and fast.

One Fomorian screamed as he jumped high in the air, landing on Cathal. Claws from his deformed grey hand emerged from the tips of his fingers, slashing Cathal across his neck.

He winced as the blood squirted out, but he kept fighting, trying to ignore the searing pain throbbing with every swing he made.

The other men to his left and right were under a similar attack. He could see his men disappearing in the corner of his eye under marauding beasts.

Cathal himself now under the attack from three of them. They slashed and cut at him with their teeth and claws. A large lump of his flesh was torn back from the shoulder as one of the Fomorians sunk his teeth into him.

Cathal let out an eerie yell from the pain and slumped over. From behind, they could hear a high-pitched roar coming from nowhere so loud the

Fomorians stopped their attack, looking around them to see what was causing this ear-piercing wail.

The leaves began to swirl up from the ground, floating around them at an accelerated pace. It tore through the Fomorians one by one, throwing them high into the air discarding them a distance away.

Creating a wall blocking the rest of the Formorians from Cathal and his men, leaving a clear path for them through the courtyard.

Cathal waved his arm at his men as they raced through the passage down the trails out to the back of the castle.

The leaves danced high around them on either side, the Fomorians running alongside them every step of the way, trying without success to penetrate the barrier that kept them apart. Their black eyes could be seen moving erratically, terrifying screams shattering the air around them.

When they reached the back of the castle, the leaves fell in behind them, quickly cutting off the castle from their view. Cathal spoke loudly, "No looking back or to the side. Just keep moving until we catch up with the others."

The Fomorians' screams began to fade the deeper they got into the forest until they could only hear the echo ringing in their ears.

Carman watched on as the leaves began to rise, and she clenched her fists, fingernails digging into the palms of her hands.

The blood dripped down her wrists as she snarled loud and wild, watching yet another failed attempt to cause any damage.

The Tuatha De Danann may not be visible on this land any more, but they were still very powerful and protecting the people, she thought to herself.

She was furious, and her eyes fell on a few of the men standing closest to her. Her eyes grew dark and menacing as she blamed these weak men for the failure yet again.

How easily she could wipe so many of them out with one look and quench her thirst for destruction for a time. Not to worry, she thought and composed herself again. Anger does not win the fight.

She waved for her sons and men to follow her as they entered the gates of the beloved home of Tiernan, the descendant of one of the people who were responsible for her overthrow all that time ago. She would take all that was special and important to him and destroy their precious land.

She glided across the courtyard with an unsettling smile etched on her face, causing Galdor's men to question their own safety.

The woman was clearly unhinged; they whispered to each other, and their promise of riches and land seemed to dwindle with every passing day.

Rian and his men had been observing the assault on Tiernan's castle from a distance in the forest and moved to the back, knowing this was the escape path their clansmen would take.

They came upon some thirty men running into the cover of the woods when they heard the wind roar and the leaves rising into the air, followed by the figures of men stumbling away from the castle. Rian quickly went to assist his friend with his injuries, and he frowned a little when he saw the marks on his neck and shoulder.

The blood was oozing profusely from them. Rian ripped the cloth from his arm, dabbing at it, trying to slow the bleeding.

Cathal looked at his friend, knowing he was a burden and spoke, "Rian, you must leave me here and any who are so severely injured." Rian nodded his head in disagreement, replying, "No one will ever be left behind, my friend. That is not our way."

Cathal was about to push the matter when Rian stood up and walked away, leaving the other men to tend to him.

Rian and two of the other men whispered among themselves. "We cannot carry them, Rian," Rian replied.

"I know we cannot carry them; we will not leave them here, and that is final." He continued, "We will take them to Mc Ulcin's house deep in the forest and leave them with him."

They moved around the men, giving their orders to patch up the injured as best they could and carry them to Mc Ulcin's home.

They quickly carried out their orders and soon moved out carrying nine men who could not walk due to their injuries.

Mc Ulcin's home was deep in the heart of this forest and was hidden from the eye of all who did not know how to find him. Rian knew if anyone could help heal the wounds of his friends, he was the man to go to.

The night grew colder as they trudged deeper into the dense foliage, every step hindered by the mud and rain. If they met with any of the Formorians in these conditions with injured men, they would never be a match for them. Rian moved at the front of the men, always alert and prepared for any danger.

Mc Ulcin had returned to his home some days ago. He did not like being in the company of high numbers of people. He was no use in a battle, nor did he travel well on his feet any more.

So the best thing was for him to hide in the forest where no one was likely to find him.

He stoked the fire in front of him with his iron stick. It blazed high and bright as a burst of intense heat hit him in the face. He leaned back into his chair covered in fur, wrapping them around him, trying to get comfortable.

His mind was weary and unsettled at the revelations that Carman was back on their land. She was one of pure wickedness, and he knew his people faced a great challenge in defeating her.

He looked around his humble home and prayed he may die peacefully here one day. For now, though, he could not let go and would stay to assist Tiernan as much as he could.

He rubbed his tired eyes as he watched the fire burn out and throw his home into complete darkness.

He did not know if he had slept long or if at all when he heard a loud bang at his door. He sat in silence, staring into the dark, hoping it was just a bump in the night when there was another bang.

This time, he reached for his sword and moved slowly from his chair. He moved towards the door. His mind wandered to the possibilities that were waiting for him beyond his homely door. It could be one of Carman's horrors: he lifted his sword, ready to swing it hard.

He knew that the chances of him surviving were none, but he was going down fighting.

Now is the time, he thought to himself as he pulled open the door and started to swing when a voice shouted at him. "No Mc Ulcin it is me, Rian!" The sword fell short an inch from Rian's head as he swerved to avoid being sliced.

He continued, "Well, my friend, you certainly still have the fight left in you. You nearly took my head off," and he laughed loud and deep in his throat. Rian spoke again,

"Mc Ulcin, we need your help. We have a few wounded, and Cathal is the worst hit." Mc Ulcin stepped back, "Hurry, bring them in," he replied.

The men entered carrying Cathal and the others who were injured. Mc Ulcin gestured for them to be placed on the furs laid around the room.

He took his Iron stick and stoked the fire again, throwing some wood on top, creating an eruption of flames lighting the whole room.

He quickly moved to Cathal's side, leaning down pulling back the clothing to check the wounds. His face fell as he called for water to be boiled and to bring him the dried moss from the table.

Rian quickly moved across the room, picking up the moss and returning it to him. Mc Ulcin wrapped the moss in a cloth and placed it on Cathal's neck and shoulder, wrapping it tight as the blood-soaked into it. He removed it and placed more moss on the deepest gash, he could see was made by teeth and no sword. His stomach retched a little, but he quickly composed himself, moving around the other injured men, tending to them one by one, giving instructions for each one's care. None were as bad as Cathal, and he worried for his recovery.

All he could do now was keep it clean, and he would try to bring the skin together when the blood stopped. He called to a tall, slim man standing by the doorway. "Go to the forest and retrieve Vervain for me in case of fever."

The man nodded, understanding what he had to do and called two more men to assist him.

Rian moved over beside Mc Ulcin, speaking quietly in his ear, "We have to leave you, Mc Ulcin and re-join Tiernan to prepare for the battle ahead."

He continued, "I will leave five able men to assist you with Cathal and our other men's care."

It had been a few hours since Aodh watched his son and friends make the journey into the blizzard to clear a safe path for the less able in their group. They were all well rested and would be able for the trek in front of them.

The storm had eased, and he felt it was time for them to continue to Ben Gorm. He called out to the rest of the men to start moving their people into the night.

The snow had somewhat covered the track. Cronan and his travel companions had etched into the ground like they had hoped. It was still noticeable enough for them to follow, only to the eyes who were looking for it.

They emerged out into the night, still lit by the brightness of the moon bouncing off the snow covered ground. Aodh wrapped his coat around his head and face as he pushed out to follow his son. The people followed, doing as Aodh had done to try to keep warm in the icy night.

This would be a dangerous night for them all and until they reached the cover of Ben Gorm.

The last man in the group was towing a branch of a tree to try to cover the tracks they were making as they moved.

Cronan, Cillian and Taibhse had been travelling with as much haste as they could. The wind and snow had been raging hard on them for many hours. Their eyes stung from the bite of the cold. They were worn out, their bodies slowing in pace. Cronan called out in an excited voice, "Ben Gorm, we are there!"

All their eyes turned to the mountain ahead, looking up at its momentous face. It was covered top to bottom in snow. Taibhse and Cillian, with weary smiles, were relieved that they had finally made it.

Chapter 17

Tiernan and the other Chieftains woke as the sun began to rise over the land once more, knowing the day they would face their greatest fight was near. For their land, their people and their way of life, which was under great threat.

The four men stood tall alongside each other as Tiernan spoke, telling them the story of a witch who had tried to rule their land many years ago and about her defeat and death.

The faces of the men grew grey in colour at his words, and they mumbled low under their breaths.

He could sense their fear growing, and he stood straight and tall with his thunderous voice, commanding their eyes to fall back on him, distracting them from their own thoughts.

They stared up at him as he spoke. "Her men all bleed and die, and we will send them back to the sea where they rose from." Their faces still showing doubt, he continued, "She has brought outsiders to our home to kill and destroy everything we have struggled to build in our lifetime, as did our kin before us." He continued, "We have banished these beasts from our lands once before, and we will do so again. Are you going to let these invaders destroy all you have struggled to create for you and your families?"

He looked at the men's faces staring back at him in silence when one voice shouted from the back of the cavern. "No! not I,"

As another and another voice shouted in agreement, soon rising to a chorus of voices shouting, "Not I."

They raised their swords in the air, chanting together, "They bleed, they die."

Tiernan stepped back with his four friends to set their plans in motion.

Fiadh and Conn's time of celebration was beautiful but brief as Dagda moved across to them with a frown on his face. "It is time for you two to leave and return to Eriu. You must travel by ship back to the shores and prepare for your fight against Carman and her sons. The door through Bru na Boinne is closed now, and there is no other way back."

He led them up a winding staircase that was very narrow, as he spoke of the days before when the Tuatha de Danann left Eriu for peace and to live as they wished without interfering in the ways of the people. As they reached the top, he looked at Fiadh and Conn and spoke earnestly.

"I am sorry our two peoples had to go our separate ways. We did it to avoid things such as this from happening." He continued with great hurt in his eyes as he opened the door into a round-shaped room full of drawings and items of the old Eriu.

"It would seem some still wish to take the riches of our beautiful land and to destroy what they can."

He moved to the window pointing out to the sea far below where a great ship stood anchored awaiting them.

Its sails were made of gold threads waving in the gentle breeze with the mask of Dagda painted on it.

They understood where they were now, and with all the extraordinary things they had witnessed, it all made sense now.

Conn looked at Fiadh, saying, "I know I should not be surprised, but I am." Fiadh replied, "I am to Conn. It is Ui Breasail, and we are seeing it with our own eyes." Conn stared across the land full of radiant green everywhere he looked, looking towards the sea that was surrounded by a thick mist as far as the eye could see.

Dagda spoke, "Gather your weapons, and you will set sail for the mainland immediately. I have word that your father and the others are marching out of Cong forest to face Carman."

Worry spread all over Fiadh's face, now thinking of her father's safety against such a dangerous foe. Conn instantly stepped forward, caressing her back in reassurance, and she smiled softly.

Dagda ushered the pair to the door and down the stairs out of the great tower as guards rushed around them, calling out orders to one and another.

As they came out onto the beach, a great bright light shining from the shore almost blinding hit them. It was a large formation of men suited in silver armour preparing to board four mighty ships similar to the one they viewed from the tower window. Fiadh and Conn gasped in amazement at this glorious sight in front of them.

Dagda smiled with a little bit of sadness in his eyes and spoke again, "I cannot leave this land as I would die from old age if I touch my feet on Eriu land again, a gift from Carman the witch when she cursed me before her death many years ago."

He continued, "I have gathered my best men to cross the sea to assist you in your battle against the Formorians and Carman." Some two hundred men stood strong and proud as they marched up the planks onto the ships near the shore.

A smaller boat with a stocky red-haired man rowed to shore, gesturing in a bow towards Fiadh and Conn to board it.

Fiadh lowered her head in respect to Dagda and thanked him for all that he had done for them.

He smiled again with a little less sadness this time and spoke warmly.

"To see the future of Eriu in the hands of you and Conn is thanks enough for me, Fiadh." Fiadh and Conn boarded the small boat, looking out at the mighty ship they were to sail on and grew excited and nervous all at the same time.

The waves lapped gently on the sides of the boat as they watched the others follow and leave shore. Many long wooden objects descended from openings in the hulls and began to move through the waves, propelling the ships out into the sea, lining up with theirs.

Fiadh and Conn boarded the ship they were to sail on, trying to take in all that they were seeing. It was not set like the ones they had seen at the shore. The men stood on their decks, covering them from stern to bow, no sails.

The ship they boarded had only twenty men, and the sails flew high. The men shouted words Fiadh and Conn did not understand.

The more the men shouted their words, it became a lulling song floating through the air with a haunting melody. The wind picked up as the sails began to flap and dance in rhythm with their voices. The ship propelled forward faster and faster as they came to the wall of mist that they could not see beyond.

The men sang new words, lower and deeper this time. The mist parted in front of them, and they sailed into the path created. It climbed high on either side, reaching the sky above and closing behind them as they moved through.

Fiadh and Conn became lightheaded as the ship rocked back and forward, their eyes unable to focus on the rapidness everything seemed to be moving at. Fiadh clung to Conn's muscular arm as he pulled her into his chest, closing their eyes to regain their balance. It seemed like forever when a voice called out loud, "All clear!" They opened their eyes, looking out ahead into the open sea, leaving the mist behind.

The ship danced across the waves swiftly as an outline appeared in the distance, casting a shadow on the skyline ahead. The sun was rising to the side, radiating across the horizon, giving an illusion of warmth in the winter sky.

The shape ahead expanded, becoming taller and shifting in their view. Its shades of green and yellow sparkled under the winter dawn, and they knew it was Eriu.

Fiadh shivered and laced her fingers with Conn's. He squeezed her hand tightly as they gazed bewitched at the enchanting appearance of their home from the sea.

Its brilliance rises from the thrashing waves on its coastline like wild horses galloping along the open spaces of Connemara.

They were sailing near Cleggan, close enough to reach Tiernan and far enough away from where Carman had landed not to be discovered.

Tiernan and the other four Chieftains were gathering their men outside the cave, preparing them for their march.

They would march straight to Tiernan's castle, only taking brief rests to preserve their strength. Tiernan knew the dangers of facing Carman without Fiachra and his men, but they could not wait any longer. Her men were spreading across the country, killing and taking people so long as they were not confronted.

Halfway through the night, Tiernan was woken by Fallon and ushered to the back of that cave.

A woman and a child had arrived at the mouth of the cave and told a story of wild demons tearing through their village, killing all in their way. It had happened not too far from Cong forest; they were guided to the caves by Morrigu.

Tiernan knew time was of importance and had to face Carman and get her to focus in his direction, away from the defenceless town people.

At least they could buy some time until Fiachra and Conn arrived with whatever help they had obtained. He stood up beside the other Chieftains and strapped on his sword, lifting the spear of Lugh in his hand and nodding at them to move out.

The men all looked at one another as they began to move back into the forest towards the greatest battle they may ever have known.

A low shrill began to arise all around them as they moved deeper and deeper into the land of the Aes Sidhe. It grew louder and louder as a great light illuminated the trees, and the ground seemed to move under their feet.

Their minds became hazy and confused as the light now was blinding beyond anything they had ever seen.

The men became panicked and confused as they tried to run, but they were paralysed. Their voices of fear sounded distorted and distant.

Tiernan knew all too well this was no attack on them and shouted for the men to remain calm and still as the light dimmed and the sound dissipated.

As they regained their balance, they could see the mountains of Umall and knew they were closer to their destination with the help of the Aes Sidhe.

The men stared wide eyed in shock, trying to get their minds around it.

Tiernan spoke up so all could hear him. "We are guided and guarded in our endeavour to win this battle against Carman and her demons, for not only our lives but our freedom."

The men became more focused on Tiernan, their minds becoming clearer as the cloudiness of their remarkable experience faded.

Tiernan spoke up again, "Move out. We have a long journey in front of us." He was cut off before he could finish when a loud horn cry echoed across the hills from the sea. It sounded out long and harmoniously a number of times before stopping.

They all recognized this as the call of the Tuatha De Danann and, with great haste, moved in the direction of where it was coming from.

Again and again, the horn sounded loudly, echoing through the air over their heads until they reached the cliff tops. To their astonishment, there in front of them, five of the most majestic ships they had ever seen were sailing in towards the sand.

The men's chatter became loud and excited at what they were witnessing. Four of the ships landed quite close to the shore, with one staying anchored further out.

Tiernan and Fallon, along with the other Chieftains, moved quickly to make their way down to the shoreline. The men stayed on the cliffs, watching a legion disembark down the planks.

Tiernan arrived at the shore out of breath and eager at the possibilities racing through his mind.

As he watched from the shore, a boat descended from the ship anchored further out, and he could see figures aboard.

He intuitively knew it was Fiadh, and his heart soared with happiness.

By her side, as he expected, was Conn bringing his precious daughter safely back to him.

Carman sat tall in Tiernan's chair, smirking at her humble surroundings of a so-called king.

A great fire pit was lighting in the middle of the hall where a partly charred body missing its head, arms and legs rolled above it, cooking nicely for her to enjoy.

King of nothing soon, she thought to herself as word came in from her forces ransacking the towns that had no protection or time to elude her.

Two women sat by her feet, shaking at her every hand movement, averting their eyes so as not to gain her wicked glare.

Dother by her side as she intended and Dian and Dubh on the walls, punishment for their incompetence.

She rose from her seated position without a word and lifted a sword, lobbing off the head of one of the women at her feet. "Horrible looking creature that was," she said and laughed. The other woman did not move or scream, only braced herself for the next cut to be on her.

Dother laughed out loud and called to one of the men to remove her. "She may taste better than she looked," Dother said as he laughed callously.

Two men moved quickly across, heaving the lifeless body and backed out of the hall, bowing low as they did.

Carman spoke again. "Brush my hair now." As she poked the woman with her sword.

The blond-haired woman jumped quickly from her place, doing as instructed. "Bring me another woman to wash my feet and make her less unsightly than the last one." She bellowed.

Dubh and Dian sat at the wall, nursing the wounds inflicted on them by their mother. They were hungry and sore looking at the women and children brought by the raids across the land. Dian whispered to Dubh, "We can take one of the women. She won't be missed." Dubh nodded with a vicious smile spreading across his pale, thin face.

Chapter 18

Gravor moved quickly with his men as they approached another village full of easy targets. He grew weary of returning them all to Carman. His mind had become enraged by the fact they had not seen any of the spoils. He thought to himself, she will never know if we take all the riches we find here for ourselves.

They moved slowly now through the forest surrounding the town so as not to give anyone a chance to see them and escape.

From their hiding places in the trees, they watched the children play, and the women go about their daily chores. Very few men could be seen. Gravor assumed they had gone to assist Tiernan. He laughed happily to himself as thoughts of gold and women danced in his mind.

He licked his dirty, dry lips with excitement, crawling in the mud ever closer to his unsuspecting victims. He slowly lifted himself off the ground and started to run towards his target, his men following his every move.

They did not scream or shout. They just stood there as these frightening men came rushing out of the trees into their town.

The women and children simply just stepped into their shelters and out of view with small little smiles on their faces.

Gravor couldn't understand why they did not look scared or run away. This was very strange. He thought to himself when he heard it.

A thundering roar was coming from behind them. The ground began to tremor and shift. Dust rose from the ground, hurtling at speed towards them.

From inside the cloud, the figures got closer and closer, the beat of the hooves thumping louder and louder in their ears. They were surrounded on all sides, swords swinging down on them, cutting into his men one by one. Gravor's men started scattering in different directions.

Their swords lashing out at everything in their path, disregarding him as he shouted orders at them.

"Stand easy, hold your position." His panicked voice was no longer heard by his band of bloodthirsty killers. Their eyes were full of panic and fear as each one was cut down in front of him.

Gravor stepped out of the street into the shadows and left them. He watched as, one by one, the men fell in the mud beneath them, blood-curdling screams and then silence.

The dust began to slowly settle, and the faces of the chilling shadows began to appear. They were just men on horses, Gravor growled low under his breath. They had been lying in wait for them and never had a chance against so many men on horseback.

He crept slowly backward into the forest as quietly as he could and left the town behind.

A white horse came to a halt in the middle of the town, towering over the townspeople, sniffing loudly, tapping his hoof in the mud, sending splashes up all around him.

A tall sturdy figure dismounted from him, patting him on the side whispering something in the horse's ear. He slowly removed the hood of his green cloak, revealing a silver mask beneath it.

The town people slowly emerged from where they had been hiding.

Fiachra removed his mask, revealing his striking features beneath.

His dark blue eyes sparkling with strength, his long golden hair falling around his shoulders. He smiled victoriously down at the bits of bodies lying all around him.

Stepping over their pieces, kicking a leg out of his way and then an arm. "Clean this up," he called out to a few of his men. "Discard them in the forest for the wolves and bears."

All his men immediately dismounted from their horses and started to pick up the bits scattered around them.

Fiachra was on his way to answer the call from Tiernan when his scouts had picked up the tracks of these beasts.

He did not understand the urgency of what Tiernan's message was until he saw with his own eyes the savagery they had left behind in one of the other towns he had come across.

The horror that they had unleashed on the people there was nothing he had ever seen before. He was not on time to save those people from the massacre they had endured, but he would not let it happen again.

He smiled at the people all around him and spoke with a husky voice, "You are safe for now. We cannot stay to protect you." He continued, "You must move into the forest and seek shelter until we have destroyed this threat." A small framed grey-haired woman approached Fiachra and took his hand before gently kissing it.

Her eyes light blue in colour, looked younger than her years and gentle as she spoke, "Fiachra, you have given us our lives, and we give you our strongest men to ride with you in this victory." Fiachra placed his hand over hers and smiled warmly, "Thank you, Grandmother. We accept this offer and promise to make our land free of any who would try to destroy it." The people began to thank each man as they ran to gather supplies for their withdrawal into the forest.

Fiachra mounted his charger in one swift jump, calling to his men to prepare for moving out. He looked back at the town as he began to gallop away, feeling rage at the monsters that had caused such fear in their land. He was ready for the battle ahead, and he would fight to death if need be.

Tiernan watched as the boat pulled into the shore, and Fiadh leapt from it, running straight to him. She looped her arms around him, her tears falling from her eyes as they squeezed each other tightly.

"Daid," she cried happily, "you are here." Tiernan pushed her hair back from her face in a gentle stroke and kissed her forehead.

"My Fiadh Fiain, you are alive. Thank Cernunnos, and all that brought you safely back to me."

Conn stepped forward, and Tiernan grabbed him into a tight embrace, "Thank you, my son, for keeping her safe," he said.

Conn stepped back as he lifted Fiadh's hand, displaying her wrist, where he had placed a bronze bracelet showing the symbol of his family on it.

It was the symbol of the O'Faolain, a wolf, meaning she was now wed to Conn.

Tiernan had wished for this day for many years, and he grabbed them both into a strong embrace, shouting to Fallon the news of their union.

Fallon cheered as the other men heard the news being spread across the beach. The cheers rose from all. "Unfortunately, there is no time to celebrate as we would like to," Tiernan said. "We must prepare for the fight ahead, and Fiadh, you must not be anywhere near."

He continued, "I fear Carman has come to get her revenge on our family. Your great-great-granddad was one of the men who helped with her downfall."

Fiadh was surprised at this revelation. She had heard stories about Carman as a child. No one had ever included her family in any of them. Tiernan spoke again, "Yes, I know, you have many questions, now is not the time."

He turned to be greeted by a tall man dressed all in silver, the glow almost blinding in the morning sunlight.

The man spoke in a deep voice, "I am Bodb Derg. Dagda sends his greetings, and us to assist you eliminate the threat that has come to our land." Tiernan looked in shock, realising he was standing in front of Dagda's very own son, and he bowed his head in honour of such a valiant warrior.

Bodb's locks of blonde hair fell from underneath his helmet and flowed out over his muscular shoulders. Fiadh and Conn had no idea they had sailed with the son of Dagda; they were amazed.

Tiernan placed his arm around Fiadh's shoulder, sensing her coming barrage of pleas to be allowed to join the fight ahead.

He was not going to allow his daughter, his only child, to be put in line of danger that was to come. He led her and the others away from the beach to the cliff top.

All the men watched their new friends move steadily with great power towards the cliff top. They knew the stories and had seen some signs of the Tuatha De Danann but had never seen any plain as day as they were now. Bodb walked tall around the men towards a large boulder lying at the top of the cliffs overlooking the valley far below him.

He stepped up onto it and scanned the forests and meadows in front of him, stroking his freshly shaved chin in thought, taking in every breath of air from his beloved home.

He had not stepped foot on Eriu in a very long time and was overcome with nostalgia.

Tiernan called to the other Chieftains and Conn to follow him and Bodb off to the side so they could build their plan.

They made their way into the forest nearby, out into a clearing between the trees. The morning was cold, with the winter sun shining bright down, causing them to squint.

Fallon had stepped up beside Tiernan as he spoke, "We have to come with a tactical attack on Carman. She is, I am sure, behind the castle walls by now."

Kyra spoke next in his gruff, sharp voice. "The castle is a fortress, and Carman knows that. How will we get her to leave it?" he continued, "She will send out her men to die until we are drained, and then she will hit us."

Bodb was leaning against a tree in the background, listening intently before he spoke. "We need to draw her out to Tooreen Bog," he continued, "her men do not know the land as well as we do, and it would make them slow and vulnerable.

Until Fiachra gets here, our force is minimal compared to hers."

Tiernan and the others stood in thought at Bodb's words, quietly muttering in agreement under their breath. Bodb spoke again. "We will stay out of sight until the time is right as an element of surprise. She will not expect any of the Tuatha De Danann to be present on the mainland."

Tiernan spoke loudly with resolve, "Move out towards Tooreen Bog and make as much noise as possible to draw the attention of our invaders. She will think we are trying to evade her, and she won't be able to resist giving chase."

All nodded in agreement and separated to give orders and lead their men to their destination.

Conn spoke low to Tiernan, "I have been given the sword Claiomh Solais by Nuada himself, or not himself in body but in spirit. I do not know if I had a dream or a vision; I simply touched the sword, and it was like I was transferred into the past."

Tiernan nodded as they walked before replying. "I, too, had a vision of sorts but of Eriu, and I was given the spear of Lugh."

Conn stopped and looked at Tiernan in surprise and recognition of what this meant.

Although Tiernan had never spoken of his family history, Conn now knew Tiernan to be a descendant of Aes Sidhe.

Only those who were of the bloodline may yield and control any weapon or instrument from the Tuatha De Danann. His understanding of everything became clearer with every occurrence that was unfolding in front of him.

Tiernan had known of the possibility that something like this would happen in their lifetime, and this was his and Fiadh's destinies.

Conn looked at Tiernan with disappointment and betrayal in his eyes as he spoke in a low, angry tone for the first time in all the years towards the man he had loved like a father. "You have known all this time this may happen, and you never saw your way to tell me, to trust me," he stuttered a little and paused, choosing his words with less anger.

Tiernan stood next to him, placing his hand on Conn's shoulder, speaking with a considerate tone.

"I did not know, I suspected, and I hoped that it was just scary stories for the young ones. I know I should have said something when they arrived. However, I was not sure this was linked."

Conn nodded, although he was feeling disappointed. Now was not the time to continue the conversation, and he would hold that for another day if there were one. He stepped away from Tiernan to find the one person who would make these thoughts leave him for now, Fiadh.

Fiadh sat quietly by the forest opening impatiently, wondering what part she would take in this great battle. Although in her mind, she knew in reality neither her father nor Conn would ever allow her to participate in any form.

Feeling a great sadness wash over her, she looked at the sea of faces of the good men who would fight for their homes and families. She knew many would die in the days to come fighting for their freedom from any outsider who threatened their way of life.

Conn appeared out of the treeline alone and looking very unsettled. Fiadh felt the need to comfort him.

He approached her, taking her hand and staring into her eyes. The shadow of what disturbed him melted away, replacing only the love he had for her. She smiled and stroked her hand along his arm as he nuzzled his mouth into her ear and kissed it tenderly.

Fiadh shivered, feeling his breath along her skin as he led her away to a quieter area away from the eyes of others. She did not speak of what she saw in his eyes when he first reappeared from the meeting. She knew if he needed to speak of it, he would confide in her.

They stopped at a large tree, and Conn pushed her up against the trunk, kissing her passionately. Her breath seemed to be taken from her as she felt his very soul pass through her.

He clutched her long hair in the fist of his hand, pulling away from the kiss as suddenly as it began. Her heart beating fiercely in her chest, she bit her lip, wanting more.

Dizzy, Fiadh searched his eyes for answers, and he slowly stepped back, averting his eyes. Her heart sank at his actions as he spoke. "Fiadh, you will travel with Bodb and his men under cover of the forest to be out of harm's way." Before she could protest, Conn spoke again, "There will be no swaying me or your father on this. You will obey for your own safety."

The words obey stuck in her head, ringing loudly and painfully through her heart. She looked wide-eyed and wounded, and Conn felt the pang of guilt and hurt speaking to her in such a way.

He knew this was the only way she would listen without argument. He gently spoke again, "Please do not feel this as intent to hurt you, Fiadh. It is important you are safe so I can fight, knowing I have someone to fight for."

He continued, "If anything happened to you, there is nothing." He placed his hand on her cheek softly, placing warm kisses on her forehead moving down her cheek.

She tilted her head back, looking up into his ice-blue eyes and whispered, "I will do as you wish, Conn." He smiled with a look of relief, placing his lips on hers and kissing her tenderly.

Fiadh watched Conn and her father move off across the fields below as Bodb gave his orders for his men to withdraw into the forest.

Her heart ached and worried would she see them alive again. The stream of men started to march out across the fields, moving in the direction of Tooreen Bog. Conn and Tiernan moved out behind them, with Kyra, Ruari, and Lugh flanking each side.

Fiadh was to travel with Bodb in the forest and out of the eyes of any possible scouts that may inform Carman of her presence.

Tiernan could not allow Fiadh to be captured and used as a threat to him or Conn.

They both looked back towards the treeline, seeing the backs of Fiadh and her escorts disappear.

Tiernan tapped Conn on the shoulder, "She will be safe, and you will be with her again soon, Conn." Conn nodded, turning his focus back to the men in front of him.

Chapter 19

Dian and Dubh slid like snakes down the side of one of the shelters that had been built by Tiernan's men to house the people brought in for safety. Now, housing the people Carman had as prisoners for her leverage over Tiernan and his men.

They had no guards posted on the doors, easy access for the sons of Carman without anyone looking their way.

Dian licked his chapped, broken lips in excitement at their sneaky scheme. They had watched the guards bring the one they wanted into this hut with two others. Dubh stood guard while Dian snuck in to quench his hunger.

The women inside lay huddled in a corner, looking up at the face they recognized as one of Tiernan's men and instantly ran to him for assistance.

He took them into a comforting embrace, sliding his daggers into the two he held at his side, cutting their necks as blood splattered out all over his face.

The third woman, hearing the gurgles coming for her companions, tried to lift her face from Dian's chest, but he pinned her tighter now into his chest.

She could only look down at her feet as she saw the bodies falling to the ground with a low thud.

Realising what was after happening, the fear overtook her and she froze to the spot, her arms falling to her sides in terror.

She could feel his chest rise and fall as the silence was overshadowed by a slow rumble rising higher and higher, and she realised he was laughing.

Dubh slid in behind them, looking at the bloody sight on the floor and hissed at Dian, "There were three. Now we have to share this one."

Dian glanced back at his brother, smiling. "You can have your way with this one. She won't fight you." He continued, "I prefer my meat with a bit of fight in them, and he chuckled as he pushed the paralysed woman at his brother. You like them dead anyway."

She could hear their words, but her fear had overcome her, and she felt like she was no longer in her own body.

Dubh pulled out his knife and, cut her clothing away from her body and stared with lustful eyes at her beauty. He slid the cold blade along her stomach and around her breasts. She shook, terrified under his touch, and he pushed her down on the cold ground, towering over her.

Dian stepped away, laughing to himself, turning his attention to the two dead women lying on the floor in a pool of blood.

He leaned down, stroking the blond hair of one of the women and grabbed her arm, dragging her body across the floor. The shadows danced off the walls illuminated by the fire burning in the centre of the room.

Dian picked up the lifeless body and threw it on the flames, smirking as it began to burn. The hair on her head began to sizzle and burn. The smell floated around his nostrils, making him inhale with pleasure as if tasting the sweet scent of a flower on a summer's day.

He could hear the grunts and groans of his brother as he shouted viciously at the woman, and still, she did nothing or say nothing.

He was pretty sure she was dead already from the fright, but his brother continued nonetheless.
Dian now turned his attention to the second body as Dubh stopped making noises, and a low jabbing sound ensued from the corner he was laying. Dubh was using his knife, thrusting it into the small framed woman over and over again in a frenzy, laughing as he did so. He was covered in blood, and his lust only grew with every stab he inflicted.

When he finally stopped, he stood up and adjusted his clothing before carrying a leg he had skilfully hacked off right through the bone over to the fire, now blazing with two burning bodies inside it.

Dubh leaned over, picking up a large stick and tied the leg to it, hanging it victoriously over the raging fire.

He stared with a demented look in his eyes, looking down at the cooking flesh blistering in the intense heat. Dubh was now hungry, too, ogling greedily, licking his lips with enthusiasm.

Dubh spoke quietly. "After we eat, we let it burn to the ground." He continued, "No one will know what happened here. Our devious mother will never know." Dian nodded in agreement.

Carman manoeuvred around the halls of the castle, investigating every corner meticulously in the hope of finding anything that would give her the key she needed. Her mind was always on the revenge and destruction of any involved in her overthrow so many years ago.

Tiernan's family line was just the starting point for her. She was intent on reaching Ui Breasail and striking at the heart of the people, destroying everything that enriched their country and lives.

"Nothing," she shouted as she tore the rooms apart one after the other. Her rage grew with every failure to locate any link to the Tuatha de Danann.

The men watched her with nervous eyes, awaiting her to take her anger out on one of them or all of them. No one ever knew who would fall next to her vicious nature, and they were fearful of her always.

Many had absconded from her ranks before, and they suffered worse faiths than death at her hands. It was safer to stay and follow her. They knew there was no real escaping the eyes of Carman and her murderous sons.

As she passed them in the halls, they averted their eyes to the ground, never making contact to avoid her attention. She knew this and was happy with it. No one may directly look at her unless she so wished.

Now, she felt a hunger grow over her. She would summon one of the men to her chambers. She raised her hand, pointing the long, skinny greying finger at one man, "You come here now."

A tallish man with green eyes and very pale skin nearest her looked up with nausea in his stomach. He had seen her from a distance, and although she looked quite beautiful from afar.

He had heard the stories of her boiled, covered body underneath the clothes and the smell of death on her breath and skin from other men.

What was worse, if he did not satisfy her, she would have him killed. He slowly moved across the corridor, following her into the chambers as she slammed the hard wooden door behind him.

The other men breathed a sigh of relief when they escaped that faith, wondering what would become of him after.

Dother grew impatient with his mother's distractions and decided to take some actions of his own. He hungered for a battle and to take anything he wished from this land.

Word had come in from their scouts that Tiernan and his men were travelling across fields away from the castle near Umaill, and Fiadh was travelling apart from them. He would take the men and strike them hard and fast. The bonus would be he would take Tiernan's daughter for himself, and he would have full control over this country. His plan all along since he saw her when he scouted ahead some months before. He moved like a shadow through the halls, no footsteps to be heard entering the castle yard.

He scoured the yard for the familiar faces he needed, and there they were, sneaking out of a side street looking as if they had done a misdeed their mother wouldn't approve of. He quickly glided up alongside them and snarled behind them, making them flinch.

"Follow me, you halfwits." He growled, leading them towards an empty shelter nearby.

He waved at two men, and they stepped up to guard the door as they entered.

Dother could smell the fresh blood off his brothers and grinned. He knew he had now a threat to hold over their heads.

Reaching over his right shoulder, he removed a lighted torch and moved across the room to the centre, lighting the fragments of wood propped up there. He could hear men outside shouting fire over and over again, and he turned to his brothers as the fire began to illuminate him.

A glint in his eye and a menacing smile spreading across his face as he looked upon their now frightened faces. They were always weak in his eyes, gluttonous and lazy. He thought to himself as he turned on the big brother charm.

"Brothers, I have grown tiresome of Mother's revenge game." They stared in shock as he continued. "I mean to take the fight to Tiernan and take Fiadh for myself."

Dian opened his mouth to speak, and Dother shushed him with a hiss. "Don't even attempt to speak when I am aware of your little game earlier, and you will do as I say. I am guessing the smell of smoke and blood off your clothing is what they are shouting about?"

Dian and Dubh's eyes darted to each other and back to Dothur. "Good, we understand each other and what I want you to carry out to the last detail." Dian and Dubh nodded in agreement before Dothur continued with his orders before, leaving the two brothers reeling with anger.

The day was moving slowly, with an eerie feel over everything around them. Aodh could see the peaks of Ben

Gorm off in the distance, and his heart was beginning to steady. He had been worried the whole way there that they may be spotted and the women and children would be killed. Alanna stepped up beside him as his thoughts wondered if Tiernan had come to battle against Carman already and what was the outcome.

She linked his arm and whispered softly, "Don't worry, my friend. I feel no great battle has fallen on the lands yet."

He grasped her hand and smiled wearily, raising his arm shouting encouragement.

Taibhse, Cronan and Cillian moved around the base of the cliffs, looking for the protected entrance.

They knew there had been an Aes Sidhe spell cast over it many years ago, and only the blood of those loyal to the ways of the Tuatha de Danann could open it.

Cillian stepped up near a large rock that paled in colour compared to the rest of the mountain base. He slid his hand along it and pulled out his sword while Taibhse and Cronan watched on.

He sliced along his forearm as the blood trickled out, landing on the surface of the rock, creating a low glow from within.

The snow slowly melted as the base rocked and cracked loudly. An opening appeared from behind it.

There were sighs of relief coming from all three of them, knowing when all were inside, they would be out of reach of Carman and all of her vicious followers. Cronan hoped his father and the others were not too far behind them.

Morrigu sailed above the tree line, scouting the land in search of Fiachra and his men. She knew Fiachra would be of great importance in the coming fight, and she needed to guide him to Tiernan urgently.

She cared deeply for the people of this land, and it worried her Carmen had returned. Morrigu knew Carmen was not just here for the mortals and would turn her eyes towards the Tuatha De Danann if she succeeded in defeating Tiernan and his people. The icy wind caught her wings, stroking them lightly, and she felt the chill through her being. Her eyes never left the ground and what lay beneath.

Out in the distance, the trees had begun to become grey and dark. The poison of Carman's presence was already taking hold of their beautiful home.

Her sorrow grew thinking about the last time this witch had taken hold of power here. So many she had slaughtered in the wake of her greed and hate of all who would deny her anything.

Tuatha De Danann was not allowed to fight in the physical previously.

Carman was of a higher power this time, and Morrigu was not going to let it happen again. She would stand alongside the people and fight.

Out of the corner of her eye, she saw movement in the trees. As she got closer, she could see many men and, at the front, a powerful man leading them. She called out loudly to them. She could see it was Fiachra.

Fiachra looked up to the sky, hearing the frantic calls from a raven above. He stood tall and waved to her to lead the way. She called out again and flew off in the direction Tiernan and Conn would be. Her heart grew in hope that they may save all Eriu and protect the Tuatha de Danann and all that is magical about their home.

Chapter 20

Fiachra watched closely from below, waving his sword above his head for his men to follow.

His head was full of anger and worry at the implications of seeing Morrigu show herself. It meant this was truly an ominous omen for all.

His men glanced at him with the same thought, their eyes bright and aware of what was to come. Some will die, if not all, and they will fight to their last breath to protect their home.

He had no doubt his men were amongst the greatest warriors on this land, and with Tiernan and Conn, he believed in their victory no matter the adversary. They had something no one had for this land: love.

As they began to gallop on top of their mountainous steeds, Fiachra could sense they were being watched, and he looked to the trees around them.

A mist floated along the grass lightly towards them with haste, a bright silver light shimmering inside it.

He felt no threat from within when the figures came gliding into view.

Many men and women adorned in flowers began to dance around them, waving their arms as they sang a melody. "We give you speed, we give you lightness, make your journey swift as the winds carry you to victory."

They danced slowly alongside them, but it was not possible as Fiachra and his men were in full gallop. He knew now The Aes Sidhe had come from the forests to bless them and assist their journey to be swift without obstacle.

The horses' hooves slowly rose from the mud beneath them as they glided higher and higher above the ground.

They were no longer touching the earth, and the horse's legs moved at a speed. Now, they were being aided by the wind itself.

Dother had gathered some of the men and the Fomorians his mother had brought to Tiernan's castle. She only wanted revenge and had no vision of real victory. He had followed her aimlessly for too long, and his time was now.

He ordered some men to show themselves around the castle so she would not suspect his plans.

They did not care who gave the orders as long as they got to make people suffer.

He was no longer waiting for her to take this land. He would do it himself, and this time, no one would be given mercy.

True victory, he thought, only came to those who wiped out all that may one day rise against him. He had no intention of leaving any Seeds of the old that would be his downfall.

His mother was distracted right now, regaining her strength. She would suck out of that gullible young man.

He watched her do this many times, and it sickened his stomach. She was truly not of human form any longer, even though she looked like one. He wasn't even sure if he considered her his mother any more.

Maybe another obstacle he would have to remove when he obtained his prize.

He stroked his long, splintery finger across his mouth as he drooled a little, thinking of Fiadh as his eyes glazed over with lust. The power he would have when he took her for his own and what he would enjoy of her until he grew bored.

His brothers slid up alongside him. They could see the determination in his eyes and revelled at the idea to destroy their enemy at long last. As they moved out of the castle of the sun, aggression was high, and they were ready for the battle ahead.

The Fomorians displayed their teeth as they shuffled out in a disorderly manner, following the brothers. Dother rode high on the Cresocia, feeling powerful, ready to make this land his.

Fiadh rode alongside Bodb high above the ground upon a yellow steed that had been brought aboard the ships from Ui Breasail. Its golden Maine fell to his knees, prancing lightly along the ground, making no sound with his hooves.

She felt lighter than air as they raced through the forest, manoeuvring through the trees without any restriction. Her hair fell loose around her shoulders, and yet no wind seemed to toss it.

Bodb glanced towards her, giving her a reassuring smile. Two hundred impressive men riding behind them in a blur to the eyes as the sun reflected off their shining armour.

Their power could be felt all around; her thoughts fell upon Conn and her father, wishing she was by their sides. She had a bad feeling as they raced through the heart of the forest, and a pain grew in her heart.

She clutched the Uaithne hard to her breast, knowing it would be an important weapon in their fight.

From the corner of her eye, she could see a flicker of figures moving as quickly as they were coming in alongside them.

She could not see what it was; Bodb moved swiftly in front of her as a spear landed in his chest, knocking him from his mount.

His men reacted quickly as more spears and a volley of arrows rained in on them.

Her heart raced in panic as she watched her guard fall away as they came sword to sword with the attackers surrounding them.

Fiadh felt her horse bolt, making a dash out into the forest away from the conflict. She looked over her shoulder, but she could only see the shadows slowly fading away as they raced further and further into the depths of the trees.

Bodb was surely dead, she thought to herself, and again, she felt vulnerable and scared.

From nowhere, a hand reached out, grabbing the reins of her horse as a giant unearthly creature appeared by her side.

A tall, frightening man with long black hair leaned down and lifted her in one swoop from her steed and up in front of him. He wrapped his hand around her shoulders, smothering her arms beneath his so she could not wiggle.

He smiled down, seeing the fear in her eyes, feeling victorious in obtaining his prize. Fiadh saw the evil in this man and knew he must be one of Carman's sons. She would not let him see her fear any more, and she stared back into his eyes as they clouded over with strength and hate.

He smirked at her obvious attempt to show her power and merely shrugged as he whispered, "You are mine now," with a low growl.

The ring of swords vibrated in Bodb's ears as he shifted his body from the ground, a thundering pain running down his chest. Although the spear had made a direct hit on him, nothing human-made could ever inflict injury or death on a Tuatha De Danann.

He strained his eyes to locate Fiadh, and his heart grew heavy as he realised she was gone.

The attackers slowly fell as his men struck hard blows on them, as the others retreated away out of sight. Bodb could see a golden shimmer racing towards him, and as he had feared, Gaoithe, Fiadh's mount, galloped up alongside him with no rider in sight. He stroked Gaoithe's Muzzle and closed his eyes, whispering softly to him.

A flash of images materialised inside Bodb's mind as if he had witnessed all himself. Gaoithe was communicating the images of Fiadh's abduction and the direction they travelled in. Bodb began to shout his orders around his ranks. Gaoithe reared his legs high as he mounted him, his mane swinging high above his head, Bodb raising his hand to direct his men.

A light of horses raced across the green meadows in chase of their attackers to retrieve Fiadh. Bodb knew time was against them, and he must catch up quickly so Fiadh would not be hidden from them.

Conn came to a sudden standstill as a shiver travelled through his soul and deep into his heart, his eyes full of fear and worry.

Tiernan turned to see Conn's face sickly white, and he knew something had unnerved him. "Conn, what is wrong?" he looked at him with uneasiness in his heart.

Conn placed his hand on his chest and spoke, "Fiadh." Tiernan turned a deathly white, his mind racing with what this could mean.

"Conn," he asked again, "What do you mean Fiadh?" Tiernan's voice now clearly shaky and alarmed.

Conn looked at Tiernan, his eyes sad and began to speak, "She is no longer in the safety of Bodb's guard." Tiernan drew in his breath, immediately knowing within himself that Conn was right.

His immediate thoughts were to turn all the men around and follow the direction Bodb and Fiadh had left in. Conn knew what Tiernan was thinking, and he spoke calmly with fortitude. "Tiernan, you must carry on with the men and complete the plan as has been made." He continued placing his hand on his heart. "I must travel back to locate Fiadh."

Tiernan wanted to object, but he knew it was now Conn's place to find his wife, and he, as leader, must continue on and save their people and land. He again must part with Conn and let him show the man he is and the husband he will be.

Tiernan held his nerve as he spoke, "Conn, go with the protection of Dagda; bring my daughter back safely."

Conn nodded as he turned his horse in the opposite direction and galloped off into the sea of men before disappearing back into the forest.

As he galloped along through the forest, his mind fought all the horrible outcomes that may have befallen Fiadh.

If she was dead, he knew if that were so, his heart would have stopped beating in that instant. They were souls joined and would be in this lifetime and everyone to come.

The rain began to fall hard and fast, impeding his progress. He was becoming angrier by the second, and his horse was faltering on the miry ground beneath. Conn knew if he pushed his steed any harder, he would injure him. He eased off and fell back into a slow gallop.

Saol's eyes were wild and frantic, as though he knew what was happening, and he wanted to keep running hard.

His white coat shimmering in the fierce rain as it splashed off him, every clod of mud rose from the ground all around them.

Conn whispered the words of calm to his loyal companion, "Turais mall a chara, beidh ár neart ag teastáil uainn!"

Saol gave a high whinny in understanding, returning the reign back to Conn.

They galloped through the trees as the rain poured harder, Conn's clothes soaked through to the bone. In the distance, shadows began to appear, moving at pace towards him.

As they got closer, Conn could make out the glow of armour Bodb had been wearing, and he slowed to greet them. Bodb slowed up alongside Conn, giving him an apologetic nod. He quickly explained what had happened.

Conn knew it was one of Carman's sons who had taken her. She was, after all, the heart of this land and would give them great power over the people. Conn spoke in a low, angry voice, "We ride until we rescue Fiadh." Bodb nodded in agreement, raising his arm for his men to follow.

A cloud of dust in the distance could be seen rising over the fields below them. Conn clicked his tongue and Saol raised his hind legs, touching down strong on the ground, gripping in hard to pursue.

Carman appeared out from the door she had entered earlier with the young man. She looked fresh and youthful for her years.

Her skin glowed a hue of gold, and she licked her lips in pleasure. She waved her arm to the men standing in the hallway.

They shuddered at the thought they may be next for whatever it was she did to him. They paused before she yelled, "Another weak soul. Remove him immediately and bring my sons here."

One of the men stepped forward, peering behind her through the door of the chamber. Inside lay the once young man. He was nothing more than shrivelled skin and bone. His hair white as snow, his eyes black and lifeless.

He nervously bowed to Carman before speaking. "My queen, your sons." He paused again in fear. "Speak, you wretch." She hissed aggressively in his face. He stuttered and continued, "They left with half of your men after you went inside."

Her face reddened, eyes bulging out from her head like a bullfrog. He stepped back so as not to feel her wrath as she screamed in an ear-piercing shriek. "Treacherous vermin is all I have birthed. Gather all the men now. We leave immediately!"

Her mind was racing in ferocious anger at the betrayal; she knew Dother was no doubt the perpetrator. He would feel her wrath most of all.

To many unreliable in her company, however, her own son was the worst betrayal of them all.

He would not ruin her chance of revenge on the Tuatha De Danann, she thought to herself, clenching her fists as her long, crusty nails cut deep into her palms.

She glided down the hall past the men and out into the courtyard to where the remaining Formorians and men awaited her, peering on after hearing her eerie screams from inside.

She called for a horse and shouted her orders as she mounted the large black stallion that was brought to her. "We ride now and kill all who we pass."

The men cheered loudly, their eyes full of hunger to cause death and chaos. Carman could taste the victory ahead of her and smiled spitefully with a glint in her eyes.

The gates swung open as she rode high and proud with her horde behind her. They were only good for fighting, useless to her when this was all over, she thought to herself. She knew how she would get rid of them when she had her victory.

The Fomorians, after becoming accustomed to their land legs again, needed no rest.

They would gain on Tiernan rapidly, bringing death on all who dare fight alongside him.

The Fomorians were prepared to wash this land with the blood of many to obtain control again. Their splintery fingers thrusting into the earth beneath them, moving faster on all fours.

Goll, as always, watched Carman at all times, waiting and knowing she would betray them when she had gotten what she wanted.

He stayed in the horde out of sight, and with no words or indication they had leadership. She would not use them to regain this land. He had other plans for the outcome.

Fiachra had ridden hard and steadily as Morrigu called out to him from the trees above.

There was trouble off to the west of them. In his mind, her words became clear. "Conn is giving chase to Carman's sons; they have taken Fiadh."

Fiachra gasped, looking at her above. His sudden change in direction confused his men; however, they followed without question. The day was growing dull. Black clouds were forming coming in from the south and would soon be over them.

They all knew a storm was brewing, and by the looks of the sky, it would be a hard one. Fiachra could see it, too. He remained undeterred and pushed on harder.

Fiachra knew they needed to catch up with Fiadh's abductors. Time was crucial.

Not long had passed when he saw a cloud of dust forming in the distance, which seemed to be coming towards them. He pulled back on his reins as his men fell in behind him and looked across at what he had seen.

He relayed the message he had received from Morrigu to explain his sudden direction change. The sturdy, rugged men grasped their swords in preparation for battle as the dust grew closer. Fiachra was ready to call an attack when he recognized the rider at the front to be Conn.

He shouted hold, and his men lowered their swords, following Fiachra to meet them.

Conn rode up fast, coming to a sliding standstill in front of Fiachra and his men.

His face strained and harsh, eyes full of darkness Fiachra had never seen in him before. He leaned in, bracing forearms with Conn, "We will get her back safe." He said with a reassuring nod. Conn did not smile or speak; just raised his hand for all to move out and took off at a speed.

Chapter 21

Carman's scouts returned with news of Tiernan marching with his men in the opposite direction. She sniggered to hear the cowardly retreat. It is not what I expected from Tiernan, she thought to herself.

Maybe the people of this land have become weaker in the absence of the Tuatha De Danann.

She was sure now the land would be easy to take, and her path to exact her full revenge was within her reach.

She bellowed out in a high-pitched shriek, "Move faster. We need to catch up with our targets and finish this quickly."

The men and Fomorians began to increase their stride as she whispered under her breath, "My highest Father, Phobos, give assistance to my army at their pace so that we may catch what we give chase to and feed your hunger for terror."

She repeated it over and over again as her men started to blur to the naked eye. No one would see them coming, and she would give back to the power that had revived her from the darkness.

Goll felt the power given to him, and he began to worry Carman may not be as easy to destroy when they had finished with the people of this land.

She has even greater power than he had anticipated, and perhaps she had assistance, he thought to himself. He would need to plan a strategy to overthrow her after they have destroyed the threat.

They moved now rapidly, as they came closer to their destination, they began slowing hidden in the trees.

Carman stopped at the front line, observing Tiernan and his men marching below them at pace. She felt a rush of excitement and hunger to feel his blood on her sword, shivering in anticipation.

They remained out of sight, waiting for the right place to attack. She had the high ground. However, if she launched an attack now, they would have the advantage of preparing a defence.

She was not going to take any chances of missing her opportunity to kill Tiernan. "No." She spoke out loud to herself, "I will wait for them to settle into camp and watch what he is planning."

She called her orders quietly, and they slowly moved away from the hilltop, blending in with the trees and surroundings.

Tiernan's mind was full of fear for Fiadh yet again, blaming himself for not being prepared for this situation. If only she had been in the castle when Carman landed, he would have sent her off to Ben Gorm for safety. He quickly shook his head, blocking out his negative thoughts and fears.

Now is not the time for regrets or worries. I must remain clear-minded and emotionless in this time. He thought to himself. He watched the sea of heads marching alongside him. Most had never been in any sort of battle ever. He admired them, knowing they would fight to their last breath if needed for their freedom.

Lugh moved up alongside Tiernan, whispering quietly. "Tiernan, I fear we are being observed from the hillside above." Tiernan did not look up and just nodded, showing he understood. He signalled to Ruairi, Lugh and Kyra to follow him away to the side.

Ruairi and Kyra moved swiftly up alongside the two men, waiting intently for Tiernan to speak. "It looks like Carman and her horde have caught up with us faster than we had estimated," continuing, "Lugh has spotted them above on the hillside."

Ruairi nodded, as did Kyra, without either looking uneasy. They spoke in unison. "What must we do now, Tiernan?"

Tiernan spoke again, "I fear the fight is going to be upon us before Conn and Bodb or Fiachra return to us." He continued. "The battle ahead will be a hard one without some of our most skilled fighters. Begin the formations of the men; we will not make it to Tooreen bog, and we must have the advantage."

Ruari, Lugh and Kyra moved off to prepare their men, as did Tiernan. He approached Fallon with a sombre face. Fallon knew immediately what was happening, and he quickly assembled their men for the oncoming attack, shouting his orders in his usual commanding tone.

Every man knew the time had come, and they moved swiftly into their positions, ready for what was to come.

Tiernan spoke clearly with great passion, "The time has come, my friends, to stop any who would threaten our home and freedom." He continued, "I believe in every one of your abilities to fight and be victorious against this enemy. Remember, they are blood and flesh, as are we. If we die today, it means it was our day to go, and you should not fear as you will earn your place in the Land of the Tuatha De Danann, Ui Breasail."

Every man's face grew strong and proud; fear and worry left them with Tiernan's words.

They knew that God would choose who was deserving of that honour on this day and fight for their families.

Tiernan continued, "They are observing us from the hillside. We must seem unprepared!"

Tiernan studied the sea of faces around him, glancing towards the three Chieftains as they gave their orders and reassurances.

Swords were at the sides of each man as they waited for the ambush Carman had planned. Once again, they had to refine their battle strategy to have the upper hand.

As a people, they were used to doing such things with everyday life, given the changes even the weather brought on them every day. They adjusted and adapted quickly with no stumbling or doubts in Tiernan and the other Chieftains.

Tiernan assumed she would attack when they looked settled into camp when darkness surrounded them, brought by the night or the storm fast on approach from the coast.

Dother moved confidently with Fiadh wrapped in his arms, his brothers riding alongside him. He could smell the innocence of her blood, and he savoured her scent with a cold, gluttonous glare. He would kill her before he would give her up now, he thought to himself, rubbing his hand across his mouth wishing to kiss her more than ever.

Dian and Dubh looked at Dother with jealousy and greed in their hearts. They thought to themselves how he always got the most precious of everything. They would, however, this time, take that away from their brother and sneered in his direction.

Fiadh's mind was racing with possibilities of how to escape. She remained silent and observed everything around her. She thought to herself about different scenarios so she could make her escape.

Never see anything as an obstacle. Always see everything with an open mind and clear paths.

Her upper hand is going to be Dother will underestimate her, and she would use this to her advantage.

She could smell his foul breath on the back of her head and his sweaty hands on her stomach, holding tight onto her. She felt sick at the thoughts of him near her. For now, she must play the fragile girl and get him to lower his guard with her. The other two would be a problem, she thought to herself.

They looked at her with hatred, and they scared her more than the horrible man holding her captive.

Her mind wandered to Conn's face and his loving expression. Worry seeped in that she may never see him again or her father. Dother could sense her shoulders slump a little, and he felt empowered, knowing she had begun to break even just a little. This was the start.

Their journey was treacherous; however, they were now within sight of Ben Gorm, and their hearts once more lifted in hope. They were cold and wet from the heavy trek through the snow. Their faces pink and sore from the bite of frost in the air. Knowing they were close to safety gave them new energy, and they moved faster now.

Aodh, old in his bones, fought the urge to sit. He hoisted a little girl with blonde curls to his shoulders and pressed on. He must always show strength, he thought to himself. The women and children looked to him for reassurance.

He looked to the peaks of the mountain and around the base in search of his son. Slowly, a source of blue light began to illuminate the rocks close to the foot of the mountain. The closer they got, they could see three hooded figures appearing from inside the glow, racing towards them at speed.

The women and children became uneasy as the older men in their company lifted their swords, ready for attack, placing themselves in front.

Aodh recognised one of the figures as his son Cronan, ordering the men to lower their swords.

His relief to see his son brought joy to his heart, and he quickened his pace, reaching out to embrace him.

Cronan hugged his father back before withdrawing and speaking. "Come, Father, I cannot describe what we have found." He continued, "You all must see for yourselves," as he ushered them forward with Taibhse and Cillian. All their eyes had a look of excitement and wonder.

Aodh spoke quietly. "What is it? My son." Reaching out, placing his hand upon his shoulder.

None of them spoke and continued to move quickly, ushering everyone in the direction they appeared from at the base of Ben Gorm.

Aodh began to worry. His son was acting peculiarly, as were Taibhse and Cillian.

As they came to the base, it seemed as though there was no opening. Cillian stepped forward and vanished. Everyone gasped in amazement.

Cronan beamed a smile at his father before speaking, "This is nothing compared to what we found, stepping forward and disappearing."

Aodh stepped forward hastily, feeling a pull-like wind all around his body and became overcome with a slight nauseating sensation.

As his eyes adjusted and he felt balanced again, he couldn't believe what he was witnessing.

The walls of the cave were completely crystallised, large pointy segments protruding from above and below.

The whole cave was lit up without any obvious reason for the brightness. One by one, the people followed through behind him, some with their eyes closed. The children giggled with excitement when they saw the magical sight in front of them.

The cavern drifted back deep into the mountain with no end in view.

There were ten adjacent tunnels where you could see openings stretched along the cavern. Off to one side, there was a stone table laid with red berries and blackberries ready to eat.

There was a warmth in the cave that was not expected, and the people immediately felt calm and safe. They gathered the blankets and started to lay them around the cavern. Tired and hungry, they ate without hesitation and settled down to sleep.

Aodh, along with his son, Cillian and Taibhse, settled down into a corner huddled away from earshot of everyone, wondering what they had stumbled into. Aodh was sure this was a sanctum belonging to the Tuatha De Danann prepared for them by the Aes Sidhe before they arrived.

There was no other explanation for fresh berries in winter or the warmth inside, although covered with crystallised rocks.

He spoke low with excitement in his voice, "We will investigate deeper into the caverns after I rest a while."

Conn rode fast in the last direction he believed Fiadh and her captors were going, his mind full of rage and worry. The wind was coming in hard. Soon, the rain would hit them, making it difficult to track.

He soon realised they had circled back in the direction of Tiernan near Torreen bogs.

Morrigu had left them a time back in search of any sign of Fiadh; she had not returned yet.

Conn scoured the sky constantly in the hope of a signal from her, each time looking more wretched.

All sudden, from far ahead above the trees, a shadow sailed swiftly in their direction, Conn's eyes lit with hope.

Morrigu flew above Conn, whispering in the wind to his ears, "They have moved back in the direction of Carman." She continued, "Carman is camped above Tiernan in the forest, ready for attack. Turn around." Conn called to Bodb as he turned Saol in the direction of Tiernan.

He knew Morrigu would not steer him away from Fiadh without good reason.

Bodb nor Fiachra questioned the turnaround and followed with their men behind Conn.

Morrigu flapped her enormous, glorious wings and, in an instant, disappeared out of view into the oncoming storm. Conn's hair stood up on the back of his neck, and he knew tonight blood would flow on their land.

They would ride hard and fast back to Tiernan, hopefully before Carman could commit her onslaught.

The rain came lashing down on them with a ferocious temper, soaking them immediately to the bones. Conn wiped his eyes in frustration as the heavy drops blurred his vision of the path in front of him. They pushed on even though their horses were slowing in the mud beneath them.

Bodb and his men were showing no signs of being obstructed by the weather and glided further and further ahead of them.

Bodb looked over his shoulder at Conn, seeing they were slowing, but Conn gave him a nod to carry on. He understood what had to be done, and soon Bodb and his men disappeared out of sight of Conn and Fiachra with a slight illumination being left behind like a trail.

Chapter 22

Tiernan moved back across the field towards Lugh, Ruairi and Kyra, their faces looking grim and tired. He sighed heavily before speaking, "Now is the time, my friends. Before the night is over, we may die, or we may live."

One by one, they stepped forward, laying their swords on the ground, each pointing inwards, Tiernan the last one to place his sword, creating a circle. They each took a knee, whispering, "Dagda, father of all, bring us strength in our conflicts. We may send these monstrous invaders into the ground and sea."

As they knelt there, the storm drifted in over them, creating great darkness around them, blurring the hills where Carman hid from their view. The rain came seconds after, rushing in the wild creating puddles of mud all around them.

Tiernan stood from his kneeling position, picking up his sword as his friends retrieved theirs. Fallon and Rian stepped up by their sides as a deathly silence engulfed all their surroundings. Orders given to all the men were to lay as if sleeping and prepare for ambush.

Everyone listened intently for any sign of the enemy, swords in hand ready. The darkness from the storm was slowly drawing over them, icy chill floating through the air.

Tiernan stared into the distance, straining his eyes to try to see through the battering rain on his face. Carman moved slowly down the hill under the cover of darkness the storm had brought in.

Her mouth watered with the thoughts of blood and revenge with a deep hunger that soon would be satisfied.

The Fomorians slithered along the ground without a sound, edging closer to the sleeping men. Carman had given orders for the Fomorians to move in first and pick off as many of Tiernan's men as they could before anyone was aware of what was happening.

The Fomorians' eyes worked better in the darkest of situations and could see the glowing bodies of heat ahead of them.

The heartbeats of their prey beat loudly through their veins, giving the Formorians an insatiable hunger for death. Their claws grew from their hands and feet, digging into the ground in excitement for the kill.

Tiernan nor his men could see or hear anything. They grew more uneasy with every passing second.

Tiernan's hair lifted on his arms and the back of his neck. He jumped from his position, ready, knowing something was nearing.

Before all of his men could react to his action, all around him were ear-piercing screams from the men on the outer edges of his company.

Tiernan, Ruairi, Lugh and Kyra rushed forward with swords drawn as they saw their men dragged away into the distance. There was going to be no battle here, Tiernan thought to himself. Carman would pick us off little by little until our force was wiped out. He shouted his order, "Stand your ground, draw your swords and fight."

The men felt terror about what was happening. How could they fight shadows that cannot be seen? Tiernan knew the men were faltering, quickly moving to the front of them and raising his sword.

Goll watched from the cover of darkness as his kindred ripped into the bodies of the men they had dragged away. He smiled happily, knowing it had begun, and soon, they would have power over these lands.

He gave the order for them to move back in for another wave of attack. He moved in with them.

He slid along the ground, almost blending into the mud surrounding him.

Swiftly edging towards the feet of a man standing with his sword drawn, twisting and turning, looking for his enemy. Slashing with his claws at the ankles, the man fell. Goll grabbed him as he screamed, pulling him backward away as his kin did the same to others.

There was a sensation of euphoria running through him as he bit down hard on the man's terrified face, tearing off his nose and his chin.

Goll wasn't here to eat right now. It was only about making them weaker. He would feast on the more tender women and children when he was victorious. His blood thirst grew more insatiable the more his thoughts lingered on the feebler meat.

Carman listened from the sidelines, feeling the exhilaration. Soon, it would be Tiernan under her foot that she would gut. Maybe she would stick his head on a stick and parade it at the front of her horde. She giggled like a little girl with her devious thoughts.

Tiernan listened helplessly as, each time, more of his men were torn away to their horrific deaths.

His heart grew troubled as he reached for the spear of Lugh, ready to use, when a voice whispered, "This is not the time."

He paused for a moment, sliding the spear back into place, raising his sword above his head, shouting. "Swing your swords; we may not be able to see them, but they will feel the sting of your sword."

The men began to swing their swords masterfully into nothingness as they heard the first scream. One by one, Fomorians seemed to appear from nowhere as they fell into their swords, revealing themselves for the first time.

A loud, frightening sound echoed across the fields all around them, almost like a horn. It grew louder and louder, dancing along the wind.

You could feel it through every drop of rain that hit their skin. Tiernan knew it was the shriek of the banshee. He had heard it once before when his wife Aoife was killed.

From the side, Tiernan could see the shimmer of silver rushing in towards them. A battle cry echoed within, and he knew Bodb had returned to help.

His spirits lifted, as did all the men's, when they saw them coming. They galloped in, swinging their swords striking at the invisible forces surrounding Tiernan and his men.

Conn could not see anything ahead as they rode in the darkness of the storm. Fiachra called to him. "I can sense death and the commotion of fighting. It has begun."

The rain pounded down on them, blurring everything in their path, unable to pinpoint Tiernan and his men's position.

As they moved closer, Conn could now hear the screams of war, an eerie wail flowing through the wind that was not of any human or animal he had ever heard also stung his ears.

They galloped hard as they rode into a mix of Fomorians and their kin, swords and claws clashing in a furious battle.

Conn finally spotted Tiernan as he cut down an enormous creature. It jumped high above him and fell to the ground when Tiernan lifted the spear of Lugh above him, and it stuck in its throat. He moved up fast alongside him, swinging the sword of Nuada with great force. Conn could feel the power emanate through his body into the sword.

His mind flashed with a knowing he was the source of the sword and not the other way around, which he had believed.

This is why only the descendants of Aes Sidhe or Tuatha De could use these instruments. He moved through the Formorians, cutting into any who crossed his path, quickly eliminating them.

The rain turned a dark red as it fell around them as if the very clouds cried the blood being spilled today. Tiernan moved up by Conn's side as Bodb and Fiachra moved swiftly through the horde of Fomorians, slashing and downing the ones still advancing on them.

Tiernan looked over his shoulder as he saw a Fomorian rise from the ground in one giant leap towards Kyra. Before he could react, Kyra swung his sword, but it was too late.

The attacker sunk his deadly teeth into Kyra's neck as his eyes turned into a glare, and he slumped forward, falling from his mount.

Tiernan called out in alarm, even though he knew for Kyra it was over, as it was for many of his friends.

Fallon rode up alongside Kyra at that moment to attempt a rescue and now was set on by three Fomorians. They ripped into his arms and back. Fallon lashed and fought.

He fell as Tiernan and Conn attempted to fight through to assist him.

Conn screamed Fallon's name in panic as he watched him being dragged away into the darkness.

Everything seemed to move in slow motion as the Fomorians picked off more and more of their friends, disappearing into the nothingness that surrounded them.

Bodb and Fiachra moved up beside Conn and Tiernan to protect them from attack. Bodb's men quickly followed, surrounding them and creating a barrier.

Bodb moved out alongside his men as they began to gallop around them in a circular direction, moving faster and faster until a wind grew. They blurred out of sight into nothing except a blinding illumination.

The Fomorians fell back, blinded in agony as the blast of light burned their delicate eyes. Unable to stand it, they withdrew towards the hills, trying to smell their way back to safety.

Tiernan's head fell with dejection as the storm subsided, and some light shone through the clouds, showing the chaos that lay before them. Bodies of their friends ripped apart and strewn across the fields, the blood of many flowing through the tracks where their bodies were dragged away.

He knew this was Carman's plan for the first attack, to wipe out as many as she could with the Fomorians whilst her main army was still intact.

She had succeeded, and they were now dwindling in their numbers between the dead and injured.

Conn leaned close to Tiernan, whispering with a sombre tone, "Fiadh has been taken by Carman's sons. She may be with Carman already."

Tiernan had no more fight in him. However, he could not show this weakness in front of Conn or his men.

He straightened his shoulders and raised his head, forcing all his fears and worries out of eyes, off his greying face as he spoke. "Conn, this is the first wave of attack. We must push all emotion away and regroup, prepare."

Conn immediately straightened his muscular shoulders, looking confident and determined, calling out to every man. "Prepare for a second attack; do not lose hope." He continued, "Dagda is with us."

The men cleared the path for Tiernan and Conn as, one by one, they banged their swords off their shields. The sound grew louder and louder, turning into a roar like thunder, shattering the silence of death that surrounded them.

Carman listened from above, displeased with their reaction to such a loss in battle. She had hoped for their spirits to be dampened. She would be able to destroy them easier that way.

From the corner of her eye, she could see the movement of many coming towards them. She recognised the massive figure as her Cresocia.

Her sons were returning to her, and they would feel her wrath, she thought to herself.

At that moment, as she was about to unleash her anger, she could see clearer now a small figure mounted in front of Dother. Her anger faded with the sight of Fiadh in his grasp. She smiled smugly.

Dother rode up by her side, lowering Fiadh to come face to face with his mother, dismounting behind her.

Carman reached across, stroking Fiadh's face, giving her a warm smile that Fiadh could tell was fake as she spoke. "You are a very beautiful creature, Daughter of Tiernan and Aoife." Fiadh looked in shock at Carman, knowing her mother's name. How was this possible? she thought to herself.

Carman adjusted her hand to Fiadh's hair, pulling it hard, dragging her to the ridge overlooking the battle.

Fiadh looked down at the destruction beneath her of all the men killed, her heart saddened.

Carman laughed, turning to Fiadh, "It will not be long now. The second wave of attacks will commence, your father will be dead."

She continued, "I was not expecting Dagda to send his precious son to help. That is an obstacle for now."

She tapped her cheek with her slender, crooked fingers in thought along her ageing, greying skin, sliding her hands into her hair as a large piece came out in her hand. The drained youth she had taken from the young man earlier was already ebbing away. She turned her face away so no one would see the unsightly changes in her appearance.

Her vanity surpassed everything, and she could not allow her beauty to dissolve. Carman dropped Fiadh's hair, walking swiftly away into the nearby trees.

Before Fiadh could react, Dother had grabbed her arm, dragging her away pushing her into the middle of a group of frightening-looking creatures.

They stared at her with black eyes that had no feeling behind them as they snarled viciously.

None of them did move towards her; however, she knew without words if she moved, it would be dangerous for her, maybe even death.

Carman stepped into the forest, grabbing a young man standing nearby, dragging him with power into the trees. He knew quickly what his faith would be, and he closed his eyes, waiting for what was to become of him.

As she clasped her fingers around his head, the pain penetrating his mind was excruciating. He could not scream. All that came out when he opened his mouth was a dull cry.

His skin quickly shrivelled like a berry laying in the sun as the moisture in his body dried away. His hair greyed as it thinned, falling from his head to the grass below. Carman smiled with delight as she felt her skin becoming spry once more, as she stroked her hair impatiently, feeling its luxurious silky regrowth.

Carman laughed, letting him fall to his knees as he glared around him, unable to see or speak as she walked away. Today, she was not able to enjoy the taste of his life force ebbing away at her hands.

She stepped back out of the forest, looking refreshed and satisfied with herself, looking across the field towards Tiernan. "Now I'm ready to face you," she shouted in a thunderous voice that echoed across the sky so all could hear.

Chapter 23

Tiernan looked up as her voice rattled the air around him. He remained unshaken, glancing around his men to check the impact.

They were looking towards the hills before redirecting their attention towards Tiernan.

He knew they were waiting for his orders, so he began calling them out. "Fiachra, Bodb and Lugh, we are not going to wait for Carman to come to us. We are going to attack." He continued, "Prepare the men for the last fight."

Conn rushed to Tiernan's side, "They have Fiadh. What if they kill her?" His eyes were full of panic. Tiernan looked at Conn, placing his hand on his shoulder with deep regret and hurt in his eyes. "Conn, we cannot think with our hearts right now. This is bigger than us. This is for the people and our land." He continued, "We must put everything else aside to be true leaders, protecting the innocent and giving them back their lives."

Conn's head fell with defeat, knowing Tiernan was right. He nodded in agreement.

Tiernan stepped up to the front of the gathered men with a stiff, resolute stance, "Now is the time. I am not waiting for them to wipe us out. We are taking back the advantage and will move on these black-hearted creatures.

Fight with every breath, knowing you are what stands between them and the future of all our people."

The men cheered in unison, showing their unyielding courage repeatedly.

Tiernan could not be prouder to lead these men into what may be his last battle.

The men began to bang their swords off their shields, chanting. "We may die on this day, yet we will die for all that is true in our hearts. In the name of the Gods."

Tiernan, Conn, Bodb, Fiachra and Lugh positioned themselves at the front. Slowly, the wind began to swirl around them as they advanced towards the hill.

Carman watched from above, listening to their chants, feeling resentful of their unrelenting confidence. It did not matter. She would crush each one of them under her and remove all that was of the Tuatha De Danann.

This land will never know of them, and she will remould the people into what she pleases. She laughed chillingly, shouting her orders as Dother, Dian and Dubh moved up to her side. "Tiernan is mine," she growled, "put Fiadh into the circle so that one can rescue her. I will spill her blood last."

Dother felt a pang of anger. She was his, and no one would take her from him. However, it was one thing disobeying his mother's orders as he had done.

He was fearful of her, knowing if she survived, he would not be able to dispose of her himself. Nodding obediently, grabbing Fiadh, shoving her into the middle of the wickiup.

His mother had enchanted it to imprison Fiadh so she may be sacrificed later. Perhaps he can convince her to give Fiadh to him. For now, he had to do as ordered.

Fiadh fell onto the thorns covering the ground. Her blood ebbed from the cuts inflicted by them. She reached her hand under her dress, wrapping her hand around Uaithne, well hidden beneath.

Fiadh knew the great fight was about to happen, and she needed to be prepared to help her family as much as possible.

Goll watched as Carman moved his kin to the front line again, nothing more than expendables for her victory. His anger rose as he watched them grow excited for victory they would not live to enjoy. He could not remove them from the inevitable deaths that awaited them without having two obstacles in the way of his plans.

He must carry on assisting Carman destroy Tiernan so he may then rid the land of her.

Their eyes were full of fire and yet calm as they emerged at the top of the hill, coming face to face with hundreds of Fomorians. Their hideous faces showed no emotion as they drooled savagely, prepared to rip them apart. Tiernan raised his sword, rushing forward without any words. A roar rose from Conn and the men behind them, showing no fear as they followed.

Tiernan swung his sword as, one by one; he cut deep into each Fomorian who came upon him, removing their heads in one fatal swoop.

He could hear the screams of his men dying around him as he searched through the sea of bodies for Conn.

Conn was standing strong as he swung his sword, taking down his attackers in scores.

Rushing deep into the middle of the horde, blood stained his face, his eyes wild and searching.

Tiernan was cut off from his men and could no longer see Conn or anyone. Carman could see Tiernan was now isolated from his protectors as she rode into the middle of the horde high on top of the Cresoica, smirking down at Tiernan as he looked up at her with hostility.

Carman spoke quietly with venom in her voice, "Tiernan, you will die at my hands this day, and the Tuatha De Danann will no longer be remembered on this land." She dismounted as the horde closed them off from everything else.

Tiernan removed his outer robe, revealing the spear of Lugh as Carman's eyes lit up with amusement and interest. "So, you have the spear of Lugh. Let's hope you can use it on me before I impale you on my sword."

Tiernan brandished it as he leapt forward, striking hard at her chest as she evaded his attack. She moved swiftly and skilfully around Tiernan. As she struck her first blow on his leg as he fell to the mud below. Her second blow swooped down slowly with determination, cutting into his back. He did not cry out, rebalancing himself before pushing up off the ground standing again with resolve.

He charged at Carman again with the spear, thrusting it at her with force, slashing across her face as it gashed the flesh from the bone.

Raising her hand to her beautiful face, she recoiled at the sight of the blood spurting onto her hands. For just an instant, she was taken by surprise.

Quickly, she composed herself, swinging her sword at his arm removing it in one cut.

He fell again, his strength failing as the blood poured from his gaping wound.

Carman's insatiable hunger was growing again as she circled her victim. "I will finish off all your men and then your beloved daughter. I will drink her blood encompassing all her power so that I may then cross over to Ui Breasail, finally destroying the Tuatha de Danann."

Tiernan looked up with his blood-soaked face in horror at her words, digging deep inside, finding one last power rising from his soul. He leapt forward before Carman could react as he thrust the spear straight into her chest.

Her eyes glazed over as blood dribbled from her mouth and her eyes, slumping over. Her long dark hair dropped over her dark features, only leaving her black eyes visible. He fell to his knees in front of her, holding the spear in his hand.

She looked at him still with hate as a smirk arose on her lips. She whispered with gurgled words.

"You cannot take me, Tiernan. However, your day has come!" Her arm swung forward with all the might she had, cutting into Tiernan's throat. He released his grip on the spear, falling over into the muddy earth, expelling his last breath.

Conn could see in the distance a group of Fomorians forming a circle away from the battle. Through a gap, he could see Carman dismounting from her beast and Tiernan in the centre.

He lashed out hard with his sword, trying to make his way in their direction, but his efforts were obstructed by his attackers.

Dother appeared from the side, swinging his sword, just missing Conn's head as he leapt back.

Bodband his men were cutting through the Fomorians, leaving none standing as the next wave of Carman's men moved in, attacking them with new force.

Morrigu was observing from above. Seeing Tiernan's demise, her heart grew saddened at her inability to take form on the land. Only the descended could step foot on the mainland as a consequence of Carman's curse.

There was only one thing she could do as she sailed down into the middle where Tiernan's slain body lay. Her magnificent wings swooped down into the centre of the Fomorians as they were thrown aside with force.

She brushed her wings along Tiernan, lowering her talons gently, picking him up, carrying his lifeless form away.

Conn was now surrounded by Dother, Dian and Dubh as he quickly re-adjusted his stance, preparing for their onslaught. They stared at him with a vicious hunger that sent shivers through Conn's very core.

They were soulless creatures. Even if they had human form, they did not show signs of any humanity.

Out of the corner of his eye, he could see the enormous figures racing towards him as they sailed past, lunging at two of his attackers.

Con-ri and Cuan pounced on Dian and Dubh as they fell to the ground, screaming in rage, swinging their swords in shock. They were no match for the sheer power of these two remarkable adversaries and were quickly overcome by them, their heads taken clear off in succession.

Dother paid no heed to his brother's demise. His mind was on the greater prize. He wanted Fiadh. Conn must die, so he may have that.

He quickly lunged towards Conn with an ear-piercing screech, swinging his sword barely missing.

Conn stood tall, his body showing its true impressiveness as he blocked Dother's sword strike again and again.

The chaos around them seemed to blur into the distance as the clang of their swords echoed through the air. Dother fought with skill as he slid around every strike Conn cast at him.

In the sky above, Conn could see Morrigu rise above them, carrying a figure in her talons. His heart grew heavy as he recognised Tiernan's lifeless body being carried away.

Dother landed a blow on Conn, as he was quickly jolted back to the battle in front of him.

The blood oozed from the wound on his stomach as he clasped his hand over it.

Dother grinned in triumph, feeling his time of victory was near. He knew his mother had already done away with Tiernan. This was his chance to take all of it.

He stalked forward, growling at Conn, "I will have Fiadh and all that should have been mine."

Conn's anger subsided, and he closed his eyes, breathing deeply. He concentrated on the whispers of the wind in his ears. He pushed all the pain from his injury out of his mind as he slid his feet along the ground, feeling the beat of every movement around him.

Dother moved quickly again, lashing out as Conn brought his sword up, slashing straight into his chest.

He fell back in pain, screaming with rage as the blood gushed from his wound. Conn did not open his eyes as he slid his foot along the ground again, poised and prepared for the next strike. Dother was furious, no longer thinking, just acting out like a madman pouncing forward, slicing and swinging crazily.

Conn stepped one, two, three strides, swinging his sword with elegance, striking hard and precise along Dother's throat.

He opened his eyes to the gurgled sounds as he watched Dother claw at his mangled neck in disbelief.

Conn stepped back, placing his foot on Dother's chest, kicking him as he fell face down into the mud.

He turned in the direction of the fight that lay around him, seeing one by one, friend and foe fall to their deaths. There was no end to this chaos, even with Carman's sons destroyed. Con-ri and Cuan were immersed in the battle ravaging the demons as Bodh moved forward alongside them in victory with his men.

Conn's mind, never far from the thoughts of Fiadh, began to run in search of her in the hope she was alive.

From the middle of a horde of Fomorians, Carman stepped forward, blocking Conn's search. She smiled smugly at the handsome young man. "Finally, I meet the distinguished Conn. Maybe I will keep you for myself."

Conn stepped towards Carman, raising his sword.

"I will never serve you."

Carman laughed, "I have already sent Tiernan to his death. You shall not beat me."

Carman stalked forward, no longer amused or interested in Conn. She was growing irate with these peasants.

She raised her hand and swiped down in his direction. Conn fell back, clutching his chest with stabbing pain rushing through him. Carman circled him like a predator stalking its prey.

Conn relaxed his mind and began to pray, *"Nuada, God of the hunt, great king of the Tuatha De Danann. Bring me light and strength in this time of battle. Lead me in the path so that I may avenge Tiernan and protect our people."*

A soft whispering began to float through his mind and in his ears. There were many voices, light and airy. They slowly grew louder and louder as Conn felt a warmth overcome his whole body.

The words Carman continued to speak were now unclear to Conn as things around him became hazy.

A light began to slowly descend on him as a shape formed in front of him. The whispers became words, and he now recognised the voice. Tiernan appeared in front of him. His eyes looked bright and warm. He reached his hand across to Conn, placing it on his chest. "Rise, my son. Nuada gifts you the essence of him. It is already within you as you are descended from him. Look deep within yourself and be true to your fate."

As quick as Tiernan appeared, he was gone.

Conn no longer felt the strike of Carman's wrath. His pain had subsided, and he felt strong, stronger than he had ever felt before.

He slowly raised his hand with Claiomh Solais lightly dancing on the tips of his fingers.

He knew from somewhere deep inside he no longer needed to use the power of his body to battle Carman.

As he had felt once before, the power he ignored was growing within him.

Carman shouted, "Conn, come meet your end, and know that all will be slaughtered after I am done with you."

Conn did not speak and placed his feet in position to prepare for their fight.

Carman stalked forward, swinging her sword hard with anger. Conn stepped to the side in a slow, confident motion as the whistle of Carman's sword brushed through the air past his head.

He swung his sword as Carman's sword collided with a great sound of thunder on his. Conn's sword deflected each blow Carman tried to inflict. She was growing more frustrated with every strike.

Their bodies matched every move the other made as they stepped around each other in fast, skilled movements.

The raging battle went on all around them as bodies fell in their path, stepping over them, not once letting up on their assault.

Carman's eyes locked with Conns as she felt a sense of familiarity in them.

"I know you!" She said with a calculated smile. "You are descended from Nuada. I remember those eyes."

Conn did not speak or falter, and he brought his sword around in a quick strike, catching Carman off guard cutting her shoulder.

Carman let out a small shriek and, for the first time, lost her poise.

She quickly regained her footing, lunging forward catching Conn's back with a deep cut.

He winced in pain, but he did not hesitate, counting his steps as he moved quickly towards her.

His eyes were brighter than they ever have been, burning with the power of his ancestors.

He struck hard, cutting Carman on the other shoulder, taking advantage of the surprise, bringing Claiomh Solais across hard onto her left leg.

She looked up in shock as he brought his sword to the side, swinging it in one sure strike as her head flew from her body and landed on the ground in front of Conn.

He stepped back, breathing heavily, staring with his wild eyes down at her as the battle around him seemed to go quiet, and the enemies stopped all assaults, disappearing into the forest.

Fiadh could not see what was happening. However, she could hear every blood-curdling scream of what she believed was her people being savaged.

Her fears grew as the battle cries slowly dulled and seemed to become distant. Her attempts to escape from her prison had been in vain. When, from nowhere, she could hear a familiar voice calling her name from afar.

She knew it was Conn, and her heart lifted with joy as she called out to him as loud as she could. She could see a figure rushing through the haze towards the wickiup.

He entered bloodied and dishevelled, wrapping his arms around her, pulling her tight into his body as his chest rose and fell in relief.

She held tight onto him as tears fell from her eyes. He kissed her forehead, pulling her face up to look at him. His bright blue eyes searched her face for any sign she had been hurt, and she was indeed really in his arms again.

The thorns had cut her skin in many places, and she was bleeding badly as he lifted her, carrying her out into the evening air.

The feeling of death was all around them as they stepped around the bodies of many.

Fiadh pulled Conn's chin to look at her again as he carried her, whispering, "My father?" Conn nodded with a crestfallen expression, and she instantly knew he was taken from her. Fiadh buried her head into his chest like a lost child, sobbing uncontrollably. His heart was breaking for her as the battle grew silent and the remaining adversaries ran into the forest to avoid their execution.

Bodb and Fiachra stepped up alongside Conn with the rest of the men as they came to realise Tiernan had fallen. They dropped their heads in honour of his memory as the men slowly began to surround them, taking a knee and bowing their heads with their swords raised.

Fiadh composed herself as Conn placed her feet gently on the ground.

She removed Uaithne from her dress and began to stroke the strings tenderly. The music grew as it danced through the wind, floating around all their ears with a soothing hypnotising effect.

Goll and Galdor had escaped the carnage into the forest, knowing they would be slaughtered if captured. They raced through the trees in search of a concealed location to elude their pursuers. Goll's plan was coming to fruition.

What had come to pass was even better than he had imagined.

Tiernan was dead, and Carman had fallen. He had no one to answer to any more. Most of Tiernan's men had died on the battlefield, making the people weak and easy pickings for his kin.

They lived to fight another day, he thought to himself and reap the benefits when an eerie sound floated across the forest.

The louder it got, the more piercing it became as his ears began to bleed. The wail of a woman in deep distress, the pain was unbearable as his eyes clouded over and his mind faded into an empty veil of nothingness.

He was overcome with what now was the shrill of the banshee full of heartache over the many dead in her land. Her voice drove them away as they marched slowly towards the cliffs nearby, stepping off falling to their deaths into the thrashing sea below.

Galdor watched on as their bodies smashed off the rocks below and disappeared.

He was alone in this land, and for the first time, he felt fear. His anger grew. He wanted revenge on all that had taken his chance to bring destruction and death. He was still alive, alone, granted; however, he could still stain this place with the blood of many.

As he sniggered to himself, the hairs on the back of his neck stood up, and he shivered when he saw two mighty shadows descend on him from behind.

He quickly turned to come face to face with two giant wolves snarling viciously. Before he could raise his sword to strike, Con-ri had leapt forward, ripping off his arm.

Cuan then leapt forward, ripping off his other arm. Galdor screamed until he could not any more. Just a dull gurgling sound could be heard as Cuan and Con-ri ripped into his body and then withdrew, leaving him to suffer a slow death alone.

Fiadh stopped playing, the wind died down, and everything around them became clearer. She whispered, "The last of the Fomorians are no more."

The bodies of their friends lay all around them, barely anything left to differentiate one from the other. Her hand tightly clasped with Conn's, he could feel her shivering uncontrollably.

The cold winter's night was upon them, and they would have to leave their fallen men until morning. The injured would need attending to first. Conn called out to the men who were capable, "Cover the men. We will return at first light to give them peace."

Conn called for his horse, Saol trotted over to them. He lifted Fiadh up, climbing up behind her and wrapping his arms around her.

Bodb, Fiachra and their men also mounted their horses, following behind them.

Tomorrow would be a day of the dead. They would bring their families down from Ben Gorm and burn fires, feasting in their honour. Warding off all that is evil and giving peace to the families of the fallen.

It would be the day Conn and Fiadh would take their positions and lead the people.

The birds began to sing, and the feeling of calm once again passed over the land.

Printed in the USA
CPSIA information can be obtained
at www.ICGtesting.com
CBHW031739150724
11608CB00008B/248